U0032423

當代中文課程

A Course in Contemporary Chinese

編寫教師・王佩卿、陳慶華、黃桂英
主編・鄧守信

二版

Textbook

課本

1-1

國立臺灣師範大學國語教學中心 策劃
Mandarin Training Center National Taiwan Normal University

序　Foreword

　　臺灣師範大學國語教學中心成立於 1956 年，是臺灣歷史最悠久、規模最完備、教學最有成效的華語文教學機構。每年培育三千名以上的外籍學生，學生來自世界一百二十餘國，至今累計人數已達五萬餘人，在國際間享譽盛名。

　　本中心自 1967 年開始編製教材，迄今共計編寫五十餘本教材，在華語教學界具有舉足輕重之地位。而現今使用之主教材已有十五年之久，不少學生及教師認為現行教材內容需要更新，應新編配合時代需求的新教材。因此，本中心因應外在環境變遷、教學法及教學媒體的創新與進步，籌畫編寫《當代中文課程》6 冊，以符合海內外華語教學的需求，並強化臺灣華語文教學教材之品牌。

　　為了讓理論與實務結合，並落實發揚華語文教學的精神與理念，本中心邀請了華語教學界的大師——鄧守信教授擔任主編，率領 18 位極富教學經驗的第一線老師進行內容編寫，並由張莉萍副研究員、張黛琪老師及教材研發組成員蔡如珮、張雯雯擔任執行編輯，進行了這項《當代中文課程》的編寫計畫。

　　這是本中心歷經數十年深厚教學經驗後再次開發的全新主教材，更為了確保品質，特別慎重；我們很榮幸地邀請到美國的 Claudia Ross 教授、白建華教授及陳雅芬教授，擔任顧問，也邀請了臺灣的葉德明教授、美國的姚道中教授及大陸的劉珣教授，擔任審查委員，並由本校英語系李櫻教授和畢永峨教授分別協助生詞和語法的翻譯。此教材在本中心及臺灣其他語言中心，進行了一年多的試用；經過顧問的悉心指導、審查委員的仔細批閱，並參考了老師及學生提出的寶貴意見，再由編寫老師做了多次修改，才將版本定稿。對於所有在編寫過程中，努力不懈的編輯團隊、給予指教的教授、配合試用的老師及學生，我們都要致上最高的謝意。

　　在此也特別感謝聯經出版事業股份有限公司，願意投注最大的心力，以專業的製作出版能力，協助我們將這套教材以最佳品質問世。

　　我們希望，《當代中文課程》不只提供學生們一套實用有效的教材，亦讓老師得到愉快充實的教學經驗。歡迎老師在使用後，給予我們更多的指教與建議，讓我們不斷進步，也才能為海內外的華語教學，做更多更好的貢獻。

臺灣師範大學國語教學中心主任 陳浩然

The Mandarin Training Center (MTC) at National Taiwan Normal University (NTNU) was established in 1956, and is the oldest, most comprehensive, and most pedagogically effective educational institute of its kind in Taiwan. Every year over 3,000 international students are trained at MTC, and to the present day over 50,000 students representing more than 120 countries have walked through its doors, solidifying international renown.

MTC started producing teaching material in 1967, and has since completed over 50 textbooks, making it a frontrunner in the field of teaching Chinese as a second language. As the core books have been in circulation for 15 years already, many students and teachers agree that updates are in order, and that new materials should be made to meet the modern demand. Changes in the social landscape, improved teaching methods, and innovations in educational media are what prompted the production of MTC's six-volume series, *A Course in Contemporary Chinese*. The project responds to Chinese teaching needs both at home and abroad, and bolsters Taiwan's brand of teaching material for Chinese as a second language.

With the goal of integrating theory and practice, and carrying forward the spirit of teaching Chinese as a second language, MTC petitioned one of the field's most esteemed professors, Shou-Hsin Teng, to serve as chief editor. *A Course in Contemporary Chinese* has been compiled and edited under his leadership, together with the help of 18 seasoned Chinese teachers and the following four executive editors: Associate Research Fellow Liping Chang, Tai-chi Chang, and Ru-pei Cai and Wen-wen Chang of the MTC teaching material development division.

MTC is presenting this brand new core material after half a century's worth of educational experience, and we have taken extra care to ensure it is of uncompromised quality. We were delighted to have American professors Claudia Ross, Jianhua Bai , and Yea-fen Chen act as consultants, Professor Teh-Ming Yeh from Taiwan, Professor Tao-chung Yao from the U.S., and Professor Xun Liu from China on the review committee, and professors Ying Cherry Li and Yung-O Biq of NTNU's English department help with the respective translation of vocabulary and grammar points. The material was first trialed at MTC and other language centers around Taiwan for a year. The current version underwent numerous drafts, and materialized under the careful guidance of the consultants, a sedulous reading from the review committee, and feedback from teachers and students. As for the editorial process, we owe the greatest thanks to the indefatigable editorial team, the professors and their invaluable input, and the teachers and students who were willing to trial the book.

An additional and special thanks is due to Linking Publishing Company, who put forth utmost effort and professionalism in publishing this set of teaching material, allowing us to deliver a publication of superior quality.

It is our hope that *A Course in Contemporary Chinese* is not merely a practical set of teaching materials for students, but also enriching for teachers and the entire teaching experience. We welcome comments from instructors who have put the books into practice so that we can continue improving the material. Only then can we keep furthering our contribution to the field of teaching Chinese as a second language, both in Taiwan and abroad.

Hao Jan Chen
Director of the Mandarin Training Center
National Taiwan Normal University

主編的話　From the Editor's Desk

Finally, after more than two years, volume one of our six-volume project is seeing the light of day. The language used in *A Course in Contemporary Chinese* is up to date, and though there persists a deep 'generation gap' between it and my own brand of Chinese, this is as it should be. In addition to myself, our project team has consisted of 18 veteran MTC teachers and the entire staff of the MTC Section of Instructional Materials, plus the MTC Deputy Director.

The field of L2 Chinese in Taiwan seems to have adopted the world-famous 'one child policy'. The complete set of currently used textbooks was born a generation ago, and until now has been without predecessor. We are happy to fill this vacancy, and with the title 'number two', yet we also aspire to have it be number two in name alone. After a generation, we present a slightly disciplined contemporary language as observed in Taiwan, we employ Hanyu Pinyin without having to justify it cautiously and timidly, we are proud to present a brand-new system of Chinese parts of speech that will hopefully eliminate many instances of error, we have devised two kinds of exercises in our series, one basically structural and the other entirely task-based, each serving its own intended function, and finally we have included in each lesson a special aspect of Chinese culture. Moreover, all this is done in full color, the first time ever in the field of L2 Chinese in Taiwan. The settings for our current series is in Taipei, Taiwan, with events taking place near the National Taiwan Normal University. The six volumes progress from basic colloquial to semi-formal and finally to authentic conversations or narratives. The glossary in vocabulary and grammar is in basically semi-literal English, not free translation, as we wish to guide the readers/learners along the Chinese 'ways of thinking', but rest assured that no pidgin English has been used.

I am a functional, not structural, linguist, and users of our new textbooks will find our approaches and explanations more down to earth. Both teachers and learners will find that the content resonates with their own experiences and feelings. Rote learning plays but a tiny part of our learning experiences. In a functional frame, the role of the speaker often seen as prominent. This is natural, as numerous adverbs in Chinese, as they are traditionally referred to, do not in fact modify verb phrases at all. They relate to the speaker.

We, the field of Chinese as a second language, know a lot about how to teach, especially when it comes to Chinese characters. Most L2 Chinese teachers world-wide are ethnically Chinese, and teach characters just as they were taught in childhood. Truth is, we know next to nothing how adult students/learners actually learn characters, and other elements of the Chinese language. While we have nothing new in this series of textbooks that contributes to the teaching of Chinese characters, I tried to tightly integrate teaching and learning through our presentation of vocabulary items and grammatical structures. Underneath such methodologies is my personal conviction, and at times both instructors' and learners' patience is requested. I welcome communication with all users of our new textbooks, whether instructors or students/learners.

Shou-hsin Teng

系列規畫 **About the Series**

Series Introduction

This six-volume series is a comprehensive learning material that focuses on spoken language in the first three volumes and written language in the latter three volumes. Volume One aims to strengthen daily conversation and applications; Volume Two contains short essays as supplementary readings; Volume Three introduces beginning-level written language and discourse, in addition to extended dialogues. Volume Four uses discourse to solidify the learner's written language and ability in reading authentic materials; Volumes Five and Six are arranged in topics such as society, technology, economics, politics, culture, and environment to help the learner expand their language utilizations in different domains.

Each volume includes a textbook, a student workbook, and a teacher's manual. In addition, Volume One and Two include a practice book for characters.

Level of Students

A Course in Contemporary Chinese 《當代中文課程》 is suitable for learners of Chinese in Taiwan, as well as for high school or college level Chinese language courses overseas. Volumes One to Six cover levels A1 to C1 in the CEFR, or Novice to Superior levels in ACTFL Guidelines.

Overview

- The series adopts communicative language teaching and task-based learning to boost the learner's Chinese ability.
- Each lesson has learning objectives and self-evaluation to give the learner a clear record of tasks completed.
- Lessons are authentic daily situations to help the learner learn in natural contexts.
- Lexical items and syntactic structures are presented and explained in functional, not structural, perspectives.
- Syntactic, i.e. grammatical, explanation includes functions, structures, pragmatics, and drills to guide the learner to proper usage.
- Classroom activities have specific learning objectives, activities, or tasks to help fortify learning while having fun.
- The "Bits of Chinese Culture" section of the lesson has authentic photographs to give the learner a deeper look at local Taiwanese culture.
- Online access provides supplementary materials for teachers & students.

改版緣起 Reasons for the Revision

　　《當代中文課程》第一冊出版迄今已六年，在中華文化中，「六」這個數字象徵著吉祥，也代表了和諧融洽的意涵。我們將六年以來所接獲的各方意見，彙整之後進行教材改版，希望能藉由教材的新面貌，答謝讀者這些日子以來對《當代中文課程》的支持與愛護。

　　新版《當代中文課程》在紙本教材方面，不僅修訂教材內容，也調整了分冊形式，便於讀者攜帶；在數位方面則改善了音檔下載的使用流程，讓操作更加流暢。此外，我們為每課對話製作擴增實境（Augmented Reality，簡稱 AR）動畫，增添教材的數位互動性。讀者只需將行動裝置（手機或平板）掃描課本中的課文插圖，就能看到生動的動畫。文字搭配動態圖像使學習更富樂趣，並有助於強化記憶，自然而然地提升學習成效。

　　《當代中文課程》編著團隊致力於落實「當代」之名，讓此套教材在任何時刻都順應潮流，符合當代語彙，符合當代中文學習者的使用需求。以此考量，推出新版《當代中文課程》，若未來讀者有任何新期許，也歡迎繼續賜教。

It has been six years since the first volume of *A Course in Contemporary Chinese* was published. For Chinese culture, the number "six" symbolizes good luck and also means harmony and rapport. We have further consolidated the diverse opinions we have received over the past six years and then revised the teaching materials. With the new look of textbooks, we are eager to thank readers for their support and love to *A Course in Contemporary Chinese* over the past few years.

In terms of paper textbooks, the new edition of *A Course in Contemporary Chinese* has not only revised the content of the textbooks, but also adjusted the format to several volumes to make it easy for readers to carry. Regarding the digital aspect, the use process of audio file download has been optimized to make the operation smoother. On top of that, we create augmented reality (AR for short) animations for the dialogues of each lesson, which adds to the digital interactivity of the teaching materials. Therefore, readers only need to scan the text illustrations in the textbook with their mobile devices (mobile phones or tablets) to see vivid animations. Based on this, this textbook is composed of text and dynamic images to make learning more fun, and helps strengthen readers' memory and promote learning effectiveness.

The editorial team of *A Course in Contemporary Chinese* is dedicated to implementing the name "Contemporary," hoping to make this set of textbooks follow the trend of the generation at all times and meet the needs of contemporary vocabulary and contemporary Chinese learners. In view of this, we launched a new version of *A Course in Contemporary Chinese*. If future readers have any new related expectations, please continue to remind us.

1. 使用行動裝置（手機或平板）免費下載 MAKAR APP （僅限 iOS 及 Android 系統）
   Readers are invited to use mobile devices (mobile phones or tablets) to download MAKAR APP for free (iOS and Android systems only).

App Store (iOS)　　　Google Play (Android)

2. 開啟 MAKAR APP
   Enable MAKAR APP

❶ 點擊「搜尋」　　　　　　　　　　Click "Search"

❷ 於搜尋欄位中輸入「Dangdai」　　Enter "Dangdai" in the search field

❸ 點擊「專案」　　　　　　　　　　Click "Project"

❹ 點擇任一專案（無須對照課數）　　Click any project (no need to match the number of courses)

❺ 點擊「開始體驗」　　　　　　　　Click "Start Experience"

❻ 掃描《當代中文課程》課本的課文插圖即可播放動畫
　　Scan the illustrations of the text in the textbook of *A Course in Contemporary Chinese* to start playing the animation.

An Introduction to the Chinese Language

China is a multi-ethnic society, and when people in general study Chinese, 'Chinese' usually refers to the Beijing variety of the language as spoken by the Han people in China, also known as Mandarin Chinese or simply Mandarin. It is the official language of China, known mostly domestically as the Putonghua, the lingua franca, or Hanyu, the Han language. In Taiwan, Guoyu refers to the national/official language, and Huayu to either Mandarin Chinese as spoken by Chinese descendants residing overseas, or to Mandarin when taught to non-Chinese learners. The following pages present an outline of the features and properties of Chinese. For further details, readers are advised to consult various and rich on-line resources.

Language Kinship

Languages in the world are grouped together on the basis of language affiliation, called language-family. Chinese, or rather Hanyu, is a member of the Sino-Tibetan family, which covers most of China today, plus parts of Southeast Asia. Therefore, Tibetan, Burmese, and Thai are genetically related to Hanyu.

Hanyu is spoken in about 75% of the present Chinese territory, by about 75% of the total Chinese population, and it covers 7 major dialects, including the better known Cantonese, Hokkienese, Hakka and Shanghainese.

Historically, Chinese has interacted highly actively with neighboring but unaffiliated languages, such as Japanese, Korean and Vietnamese. The interactions took place in such areas as vocabulary items, phonological structures, a few grammatical features and most importantly the writing script.

Typological Features of Chinese

Languages in the world are also grouped together on the basis of language characteristics, called language typology. Chinese has the following typological traits, which highlight the dissimilarities between Chinese and English.

A. Chinese is a non-tense language. Tense is a grammatical device such that the verb changes according to the time of the event in relation to the time of utterance. Thus 'He talks nonsense' refers to his habit, while 'He talked nonsense' refers to a time in the past when he behaved that way, but he does not necessarily do that all the time. 'Talked' then is a verb in the past tense. Chinese does not operate with this device but marks the time of events with time expressions such as 'today' or 'tomorrow' in the sentence. The verb remains the same regardless of time of happening. This type of language is labeled as an atensal language, while English and most European languages are tensal languages. Knowing this particular trait can help European learners of Chinese avoid mistakes to do with verbs in Chinese. Thus, in responding to 'What did you do in China last year?' Chinese is 'I teach English (last year)'; and to 'What are you doing now in Japan?' Chinese is again 'I teach English (now)'.

B. Nouns in Chinese are not directly countable. Nouns in English are either countable, e.g. 2 candies, or non-countable, e.g. *2 salts, while all nouns in Chinese are non-countable. When they are to be counted, a measure, or called classifier, must be used between a noun and a number, e.g. 2-piece-candy. Thus, Chinese is a classifier language. Only non-countable nouns in English are used with measures, e.g. a drop of water.

Therefore it is imperative to learn nouns in Chinese together with their associated measures/classifiers. There are only about 30 high-frequency measures/classifiers in Chinese to be mastered at the initial stage of learning.

C. Chinese is a Topic-Prominent language. Sentences in Chinese quite often begin with somebody or something that is being talked about, rather than the subject of the verb in the sentence. This item is called a topic in linguistics. Most Asian languages employ topic, while most European languages employ subject. The following bad English sentences, sequenced below per frequency of usage, illustrate the topic structures in Chinese.

*Senator Kennedy, people in Europe also respected.

*Seafood, Taiwanese people love lobsters best.

*President Obama, he attended Harvard University.

Because of this feature, Chinese people tend to speak 'broken' English, whereas English speakers tend to sound 'complete', if bland and alien, when they talk in Chinese. Through practice and through keen observations of what motivates the use of a topic in Chinese, this feature of Chinese can be acquired eventually.

D. Chinese tends to drop things in the sentence. The 'broken' tendencies mentioned above also include not using nouns in a sentence where English counterparts are 'complete'. This tendency is called dropping, as illustrated below through bad English sentences.

Are you coming tomorrow? ----- *Come!

What did you buy? ----- *Buy some jeans.

*This bicycle, who rides? ----- *My old professor rides.

The 1st example drops everything except the verb, the 2nd drops the subject, and the 3rd drops the object. Dropping happens when what is dropped is easily recoverable or identifiable from the contexts or circumstances. Not doing this, Europeans are often commented upon that their sentences in Chinese are too often inundated with unwanted pronouns!!

Phonological Characteristics of Chinese

Phonology refers to the system of sound, the pronunciation, of a language. To untrained ears, Chinese language sounds unfamiliar, sort of alien in a way. This is due to the fact that Chinese sound system contains some elements that are not part of the sound systems of European languages, though commonly found on the Asian continent. These features will be explained below.

On the whole, the Chinese sound system is not really very complicated. It has 7 vowels, 5 of which are found in English (i, e, a, o, u), plus 2 which are not (-e,); and it has 21 consonants, 15 of which are quite common, plus 6 which are less common (zh, ch, sh, r, z, c). And Chinese has a fairly simple syllable shape, i.e. consonant + vowel plus possible nasals (n or ng). What is most striking to English speakers is that every syllable in Chinese has a 'tone', as will be detailed directly below. But, a word on the sound representation, the pinyin system, first.

A. Hanyu Pinyin. Hanyu Pinyin is a variety of Romanization systems that attempt to represent the sound of Chinese through the use of Roman letters (abc...). Since the end of the 19th century, there have been about half a dozen Chinese Romanization systems, including the Wade-Giles, Guoyu Luomazi, Yale, Hanyu Pinyin, Lin Yutang, and Zhuyin Fuhao Di'ershi, not to mention the German system, the French system etc. Thanks to the consensus of media worldwide, and through the support of the UN, Hanyu Pinyin has become the standard worldwide. Taiwan is probably the only place in the world that does not support nor employ Hanyu Pinyin. Instead, it uses non-Roman symbols to represent the sound, called Zhuyin Fuhao, alias BoPoMoFo (cf. the symbols employed in this volume). Officially, that is. Hanyu Pinyin represents the Chinese sound as follows.

b, p, m, f   d, t, n, l   g, k, h   j, q, x   zh, ch, sh, r   z, c, s

a, o, -e, e   ai, ei, ao, ou   an, en, ang, eng   -r, i, u, ü

B. Chinese is a tonal language. A tone refers to the voice pitch contour. Pitch contours are used in many languages, including English, but for different functions in different languages. English uses them to indicate the speaker's viewpoints, e.g. 'well' in different contours may indicate impatience, surprise, doubt etc. Chinese, on the other hand, uses contours to refer to different meanings, words. Pitch contours with different linguistic functions are not transferable from one language to another. Therefore, it would be futile trying to learn Chinese tones by looking for or identifying their contour counterparts in English.

Mandarin Chinese has 4 distinct tones, the fewest among all Han dialects, i.e. level, rising, dipping and falling, marked ˉ ˊ ˇ ˋ, and it has only one tone-change rule, i.e. ˇ ˇ → ˊ ˇ, though the conditions for this change are fairly complicated. In addition to the four tones, Mandarin also has one neutral(ized) tone, i.e.□, pronounced short/unstressed, which is derived, historically if not synchronically, from the 4 tones; hence the term neutralized. Again, the conditions and environments for the neutralization are highly complex and cannot be explored in this space.

C. Syllable final −r effect (vowel retroflexivisation). The northern variety of Hanyu, esp. in Beijing, is known for its richness in the −r effect at the end of a syllable. For example, 'flower' is 'huā' in southern China but 'huār' in Beijing. Given the prominence of the city Beijing, this sound feature tends to be defined as standard nationwide; but that −r effect is rarely attempted in the south. There do not seem to be rigorous rules governing what can and what cannot take the −r effect. It is thus advised that learners of Chinese resort to rote learning in this case, as probably even native speakers of northern Chinese do.

D. Syllables in Chinese do not 'connect'. 'Connect' here refers to the merging of the tail of a syllable with the head of a subsequent syllable, e.g. English pronounces 'at' + 'all' as 'at+tall', 'did' +'you' as 'did+dyou' and 'that'+'is' as 'that+th'is'. On the other hand, syllables in Chinese are isolated from each other and do not connect in this way. Fortunately, this is not a serious problem for English language learners, as the syllable structures in Chinese are rather limited, and there are not many candidates for this merging. We noted above that Chinese syllables take the form of CV plus possible 'n' and 'ng'. CV does not give rise to connecting, not even in English; so be extra cautious when a syllable ends with 'n' or 'g' and a subsequent syllable begins with a V, e.g. MǐnÀo 'Fujian Province and Macao'. Nobody would understand 'min+nao'!!

E. Retroflexive consonants. 'Retroflexive' refers to consonants that are pronounced with the tip of the tongue curled up (-flexive) backwards (retro-). There are altogether 4 such consonants, i.e. zh, ch, sh, and r. The pronunciation of these consonants reveals the geographical origin of native Chinese speakers. Southerners do not have them, merging them with z, c, and s, as is commonly observed in Taiwan. Curling up of the tongue comes in various degrees. Local Beijing dialect is well known for its prominent curling. Imagine curling up the tongue at the beginning of a syllable and curling it up again for the –r effect!! ! Try 'zhèr-over here', 'zhuōr-table' and 'shuǐr-water'.

On Chinese Grammar

'Grammar' refers to the ways and rules of how words are organized into a string that is a sentence in a language. Given the fact that all languages have sentences, and at the same time non-sentences, all languages including Chinese have grammar. In this section, the most salient and important features and issues of Chinese grammar will be presented, but a summary of basic structures, as referenced against English, is given first.

A. Similarities in Chinese and English.

	English	Chinese
SVO	They sell coffee.	Tāmen mài kāfēi.
AuxV+Verb	You may sit down!	Nǐ kěyǐ zuòxià ō!
Adj+Noun	sour grapes	suān pútáo
Prep+its Noun	at home	zài jiā
Num+Meas+Noun	a piece of cake	yí kuài dàngāo
Demons+Noun	those students	nàxiē xuéshēng

B. Dissimilar structures.

	English	Chinese
RelClause: Noun	the book that you bought	nǐ mǎi de shū
VPhrase: PrepPhrase	to eat at home	zài jiā chīfàn
Verb: Adverbial	Eat slowly!	Mànmār chī!

Set: Subset	6th Sept, 1967	1967 nián 9 yuè 6 hào
	Taipei, Taiwan	Táiwān Táiběi
	3 of my friends…	wǒ de péngyǒu, yǒu sān ge…

C. Modifier precedes modified (MPM). This is one of the most important grammatical principles in Chinese. We see it operating actively in the charts given above, so that adjectives come before nouns they modify, relative clauses also come before the nouns they modify, possessives come before nouns (tā de diànnǎo 'his computer'), auxiliary verbs come before verbs, adverbial phrases before verbs, prepositional phrases come before verbs etc. This principle operates almost without exceptions in Chinese, while in English modifiers sometimes precede and some other times follow the modified.

D. Principle of Temporal Sequence (PTS). Components of a sentence in Chinese are lined up in accordance with the sequence of time. This principle operates especially when there is a series of verbs contained within a sentence, or when there is a sentential conjunction. First compare the sequence of 'units' of an event in English and that in its Chinese counterpart.

Event: David /went to New York/ by train /from Boston/ to see his sister.

English:	1	2	3	4	5
Chinese:	1	4	2	3	5

Now in real life, David got on a train, the train departed from Boston, it arrived in New York, and finally he visited his sister. This sequence of units is 'natural' time, and the Chinese sentence 'Dàwèi zuò huǒchē cóng Bōshìdùn dào Niǔyuē qù kàn tā de jiějie' follows it, but not English. In other words, Chinese complies strictly with PTS.

When sentences are conjoined, English has various possibilities in organizing the conjunction. First, the scenario. H1N1 hits China badly (event-1), and as a result, many schools were closed (event-2). Now, English has the following possible ways of conjoining to express this, e.g.

Many schools were closed, because/since H1N1 hit China badly. (E2+E1)

H1N1 hit China badly, so many schools were closed. (E1+E2)

As H1N1 hit China badly, many schools were closed. (E1+E2)

Whereas the only way of expressing the same in Chinese is E1+E2 when both conjunctions are used (yīnwèi…suǒyǐ…), i.e.

Zhōngguó yīnwèi H1N1 gǎnrǎn yánzhòng (E1), suǒyǐ xǔduō xuéxiào zhànshí guānbì (E2).

PTS then helps explain why 'cause' is always placed before 'consequence' in Chinese.

PTS is also seen operating in the so-called verb-complement constructions in Chinese, e.g. shā-sǐ 'kill+dead', chī-bǎo 'eat+full', dǎ-kū 'hit+cry' etc. The verb represents an action that must have happened first before its consequence.

There is an interesting group of adjectives in Chinese, namely 'zǎo-early', 'wǎn-late', 'kuài-fast', 'màn-slow', 'duō-plenty', and 'shǎo-few', which can be placed either before (as adverbials) or after (as complements) of their associated verbs, e.g.

Nǐ míngtiān zǎo diǎr lái! (Come earlier tomorrow!)

Wǒ lái zǎo le. Jìnbúqù. (I arrived too early. I could not get in.)

When 'zǎo' is placed before the verb 'lái', the time of arrival is intended, planned, but when it is placed after, the time of arrival is not pre-planned, maybe accidental. The difference complies with PTS. The same difference holds in the case of the other adjectives in the group, e.g.

Qǐng nǐ duō mǎi liǎngge! (Please get two extra!)

Wǒ mǎiduō le. Zāotà le! (I bought two too many. Going to be wasted!)

'Duō' in the first sentence is going to be pre-planned, a pre-event state, while in the second, it's a post-event report. Pre-event and post-event states then are naturally taken care of by PTS. Our last set in the group is more complicated. 'Kuài' and 'màn' can refer to amount of time in addition to manner of action, as illustrated below.

Nǐ kuài diǎr zǒu; yào chídào le! (Hurry up and go! You'll be late (e.g. for work)!)

Qǐng nǐ zǒu kuài yìdiǎr! (Please walk faster!)

'Kuài' in the first can be glossed as 'quick, hurry up' (in as little time as possible after the utterance), while that in the second refers to manner of walking. Similarly, 'màn yìdiǎr zǒu-don't leave yet' and 'zǒu màn yìdiǎr-walk more slowly'.

We have seen in this section the very important role in Chinese grammar played by variations in word-order. European languages exhibit rich resources in changing the forms of verbs, adjectives and nouns, and Chinese, like other Asian languages, takes great advantage of word-order.

E. Where to find subjects in existential sentences. Existential sentences refer to sentences in which the verbs express appearing (e.g. coming), disappearing (e.g. going) and presence (e.g. written (on the wall)). The existential verbs are all intransitive, and thus they are all associated with a subject, without any objects naturally. This type of sentences deserves a mention in this introduction, as they exhibit a unique structure in Chinese. When their subjects are in definite reference (something that can be referred to, e.g. pronouns and nouns with definite article in English) the subject appears at the front of the sentence, i.e. before the existential verb, but when their subjects are in indefinite reference (nothing in particular), the subject appears after the verb. Compare the following pair of sentences in Chinese against their counterparts in English.

Kèrén dōu lái le. Chīfàn ba! (All the guests we invited have arrived. Let's serve the dinner.)

Duìbùqǐ! Láiwǎn le. Jiālǐ láile yí ge kèrén. (Sorry for being late! I had an (unexpected) guest.)

More examples of post-verbal subjects are given below.

Zhè cì táifēng sǐle bù shǎo rén. (Quite a few people died during the typhoon this time.)

Zuótiān wǎnshàng xiàle duō jiǔ de yǔ? (How long did it rain last night?)

Zuótiān wǎnshàng pǎole jǐ ge fànrén? (How many inmates got away last night?)

Chēzi lǐ zuòle duōshǎo rén a? (How many people were in the car?)

Exactly when to place the existential subject after the verb will remain a challenge for learners of Chinese for quite a significant period of time. Again, observe and deduce!! Memorising sentence by sentence would not help!!

The existential subjects presented above are simple enough, e.g. people, a guest, rain and inmates. But when the subject is complex, further complications emerge!! A portion of the complex subject stays in front of the verb, and the remaining goes to the back of the verb, e.g.

Míngtiān nǐmen qù jǐge rén? (How many of you will be going tomorrow?)

Wǒ zuìjìn diàole bù shǎo tóufǎ. (I lost=fell quite a lot of hair recently.)

Qùnián dìzhèn, tā sǐle sān ge gēge. (He lost=died 3 brothers during the earthquake last year.)

In linguistics, we say that existential sentences in Chinese have a lot of semantic and information structures involved.

F. A tripartite system of verb classifications in Chinese. English has a clear division between verbs and adjectives, but the boundary in Chinese is quite blurred, which quite seriously misleads English-speaking learners of Chinese. The error in *Wǒ jīntiān shì máng. 'I am busy today.' is a daily observation in Chinese 101! Why is it a common mistake for beginning learners? What do our textbooks and/or teachers do about it, so that the error is discouraged, if not suppressed? Nothing, much! What has not been realized in our profession is that Chinese verb classification is more strongly semantic, rather than more strongly syntactic as in English.

Verbs in Chinese have 3 sub-classes, namely Action Verbs, State Verbs and Process Verbs. Action Verbs are time-sensitive activities (beginning and ending, frozen with a snap-shot, prolonged), are will-controlled (consent or refuse), and usually take human subjects, e.g. 'chī-eat', 'mǎi-buy' and 'xué-learn'. State Verbs are non-time-sensitive physical or mental states, inclusive of the all-famous adjectives as a further sub-class, e.g. 'ài-love', 'xīwàng-hope' and 'liàng-bright'. Process Verbs refer to instantaneous change from one state to another, 'sǐ-die', 'pò-break, burst' and 'wán-finish'.

The new system of parts of speech in Chinese as adopted in this series is built on this very foundation of this tripartite verb classification. Knowing this new system will be immensely helpful in learning quite a few syntactic structures in Chinese that are nicely related to the 3 classes of verbs, as will be illustrated with negation in Chinese in the section below.

The table below presents some of the most important properties of these 3 classes of verbs, as reflected through syntactic behaviour.

	Action Verbs	State Verbs	Process Verbs
Hěn- modification	✗	✓	✗
Le- completive	✓	✗	✓
Zài- progressive	✓	✗	✗
Reduplication	✓ (tentative)	✓ (intensification)	✗
Bù- negation	✓	✓	✗
Méi- negation	✓	✗	✓

Here are more examples of 3 classes of verbs.

Action Verbs: mǎi 'buy', zuò 'sit', xué 'learn; imitate', kàn 'look'

State Verbs: xǐhuān 'like', zhīdào 'know', néng 'can', guì 'expensive'

Process Verbs: wàngle 'forget', chén 'sink', bìyè 'graduate', xǐng 'wake up'

G. Negation. Negation in Chinese is by means of placing a negative adverb immediately in front of a verb. (Remember that adjectives in Chinese are a type of State verbs!) When an action verb is negated with 'bu', the meaning can be either 'intend not to, refuse to' or 'not in a habit of', e.g.

Nǐ bù mǎi piào; wǒ jiù bú ràng nǐ jìnqù! (If you don't buy a ticket, I won't let you in!)

Tā zuótiān zhěng tiān bù jiē diànhuà. (He did not want to answer the phone all day yesterday.)

Dèng lǎoshī bù hē jiǔ. (Mr. Teng does not drink.)

'Bù' has the meaning above but is independent of temporal reference. The first sentence above refers to the present moment or a minute later after the utterance, and the second to the past. A habit again is panchronic. But when an action verb is negated with 'méi(yǒu)', its time reference must be in the past, meaning 'something did not come to pass', e.g.

Tā méi lái shàngbān. (He did not come to work.)

Tā méi dài qián lái. (He did not bring any money.)

A state verb can only be negated with 'bù', referring to the non-existence of that state, whether in the past, at present, or in the future, e.g.

Tā bù zhīdào zhèjiàn shì. (He did not/does not know this.)

Tā bù xiǎng gēn nǐ qù. (He did not/does not want to go with you.)

Niǔyuē zuìjìn bú rè. (New York was/is/will not be hot.)

A process verb can only be negated with 'méi', referring to the non-happening of a change from one state to another, usually in the past, e.g.

Yīfú méi pò; nǐ jiù rēng le? (You threw away perfectly good clothes?)

Niǎo hái méi sǐ; nǐ jiù fàng le ba! (The bird is still alive. Why don't you let it free?)

Tā méi bìyè yǐqián, hái děi dǎgōng. (He has to work odd jobs before graduating.)

As can be gathered from the above, negation of verbs in Chinese follows neat patterns, but this is so only after we work with the new system of verb classifications as presented in this series. Here's one more interesting fact about negation in Chinese before closing this section. When some action verbs refer to some activities that result in something stable, e.g. when you put on clothes, you want the clothes to stay on you, the negation of those verbs can be usually translated in the present tense in English, e.g.

Tā zěnme méi chuān yīfú? (How come he is naked?)

Wǒ jīntiān méi dài qián. (I have no money with me today.)

H. A new system of Parts of Speech in Chinese. In the system of parts of speech adopted in this series, there are at the highest level a total of 8 parts of speech, as given below. This system includes the following major properties. First and foremost, it is errors-driven and can address some of the most prevailing errors exhibited by learners of Chinese. This characteristic dictates the depth of sub-categories in a system of grammatical categories. Secondly, it employs the concept of 'default'. This property greatly simplifies the over-all framework of the new system, so that it reduces the number of categories used, simplifies the labeling of categories, and takes advantage of the learners' contribution in terms of positive transfer. And lastly, it incorporates both semantic as well as syntactic concepts, so that it bypasses the traditionally problematic category of adjectives by establishing three major semantic types of verbs, viz. action, state and process.

Adv	Adverb (dōu 'all', dàgài 'probably')
Conj	Conjunction (gēn 'and', kěshì 'but')
Det	Determiner (zhè 'this', nà 'that')
M	Measure (ge, tiáo; xià, cì)
N	Noun (wǒ 'I', yǒngqì 'courage')
Ptc	Particle (ma 'question particle', le 'completive verbal particle')
Prep	Preposition (cóng 'from', duìyú 'regarding')
V	Action Verb, transitive (mǎi 'buy', chī 'eat')
Vi	Action Verb, intransitive (kū 'cry', zuò 'sit')
Vaux	Auxiliary Verb (néng 'can', xiǎng 'would like to')
V-sep	Separable Verb (jiéhūn 'get married', shēngqì 'get angry')
Vs	State Verb, intransitive (hǎo 'good', guì 'expensive')
Vst	State Verb, transitive (xǐhuān 'like', zhīdào 'know')
Vs-attr	State Verb, attributive (zhǔyào 'primary', xiùzhēn 'mini-')
Vs-pred	State Verb, predicative (gòu 'enough', duō 'plenty')
Vp	Process Verb, intransitive (sǐ 'die', wán 'finish')
Vpt	Process Verb, transitive (pò (dòng) 'lit. break (hole) , liè (fèng) 'lit. crack (a crack))

Notes:

Default values: When no marking appears under a category, a default reading takes place, which has been built into the system by observing the commonest patterns of the highest frequency. A default value can be loosely understood as the most likely candidate. A default system results in using fewer symbols, which makes it easy on the eyes, reducing the amount of processing. Our default readings are as follows.

Default transitivity. When a verb is not marked, i.e. V, it's an action verb. An unmarked action verb, furthermore, is transitive. A state verb is marked as Vs, but if it's not further marked, it's intransitive. The same holds for process verbs, i.e. Vp is by default intransitive.

Default position of adjectives. Typical adjectives occur as predicates, e.g. 'This is great!' Therefore, unmarked Vs are predicative, and adjectives that cannot be predicates will be marked for this feature, e.g. zhǔyào 'primary' is an adjective but it cannot be a predicate, i.e. *Zhètiáo lù hěn zhǔyào. '*This road is very primary.' Therefore it is marked Vs-attr, meaning it can only be used attributively, i.e. zhǔyào dàolù 'primary road'. On the other hand, 'gòu' 'enough' in Chinese can only be used predicatively, not attributively, e.g. 'Shíjiān gòu' '*?Time is enough.', but not *gòu shíjiān 'enough time'. Therefore gòu is marked Vs-pred. Employing this new system of parts of speech guarantees good grammar!

Default wordhood. In English, words cannot be torn apart and be used separately, e.g. *mis- not – understand. Likewise in Chinese, e.g. *xǐbùhuān 'do not like'. However, there is a large group of words in Chinese that are exceptions to this probably universal rule and can be separated. They are called 'separable words', marked -sep in our new system of parts of speech. For example, shēngqì 'angry' is a word, but it is fine to say *shēng tā qì* 'angry at him'. Jiéhūn 'get married' is a word but it's fine to say *jiéguòhūn* 'been married before' or *jiéguò sān cì hūn* 'been married 3 times before'. There are at least a couple of hundred separable words in modern Chinese. Even native speakers have to learn that certain words can be separated. Thus, memorizing them is the only way to deal with them by learners, and our new system of parts of speech helps them along nicely. Go over the vocabulary lists in this series and look for the marking –sep.

Now, what motivates this severing of words? Ask Chinese gods, not your teachers! We only know a little about the syntactic circumstances under which they get separated. First and foremost, separable words are in most cases intransitive verbs, whether action, state or process. When these verbs are further associated with targets (nouns, conceptual objects), frequency (number of times), duration (for how long), occurrence (done, done away with) etc., separation takes pace and these associated elements are inserted in between. More examples are given below.

Wǒ jīnnián yǐjīng *kǎo*guò 20 cì *shì* le!! (I've taken 20 exams to date this year!)

Wǒ *dào*guò *qiàn* le; tā hái shēngqì! (I apologized, but he's still mad!)

Fàng sān tiān *jià*; dàjiā dōu zǒu le. (There will be a break of 3 days, and everyone has left.)

Final Words

This is a very brief introduction to the modern Mandarin Chinese language, which is the standard world-wide. This introduction can only highlight the most salient properties of the language. Many other features of the language have been left out by design. For instance, nothing has been said about the patterns of word-formations in Chinese, and no presentation has been made of the unique written script of the language. Readers are advised to search on-line for resources relating to particular aspects of the language. For reading, please consult a highly readable best-seller in this regard, viz. Li, Charles and Sandra Thompson. 1982. Mandarin Chinese: a reference grammar. UC Los Angeles Press. (Authorised reprinting by Crane publishing Company, Taipei, Taiwan, still available as of October 2009).

Highlights of Lessons

各課重點

Lessons	Topic & Themes	Learning Objectives	Grammar

1
Welcome to Taiwan!
	Introducing myself	1. Learning simple greetings.
		2. Learning simple phrases to introduce people.
		3. Learning simple phrases to discuss likes/dislikes.
		4. Learning simple phrases to express gratitude.
			1. Ways to Ask Questions in Chinese
			  A. Asking a Questions with A-not-A
			  B. Asking Questions with 嗎 ma
			2. Answering Questions in Chinese
			  A. Affirmative Answers
			  B. Negative Replies with 不 bù
			3. Modification Marker 很 hěn
			4. Contrastive Questions with 呢 ne

2 My Family	Family members	1. Learning to talk about people in my family members and their names. 2. Learning to describe people, places, and possessions. 3. Learning to talk about the number of people in a family.	1. 的 de *possessive* 2. Modifier Marker 的 de 3. 有 yǒu *possessive* 4. 都 dōu *totality* 5. Measures 個 ge and 張 zhāng
3 What Are You Doing Over the Weekend?	Hobbies	1. Learning to describe likes/dislikes (e.g., sports and movies). 2. Learning to express what two groups have in common. 3. Learning to politely ask others their opinions and make simple suggestions. 4. Learning to form choice questions.	1. Placement of Time Words 2. To Go Do Something with 去 qù 3. Topic Sentences 4. The Word Order of Adverbs 也 yě, 都 dōu and 常 cháng 5. Making Suggestions 吧 ba
4 Excuse Me. How Much Does That Cost in Total?	Shopping	1. Learning to ask and talk about prices. 2. Learning to ask for reasons. 3. Learning to use simple phrases to describe the size and function of common objects.	1. Measures 塊 kuài, 杯 bēi, 支 zhī and 種 zhǒng 2. Preposition 幫 bāng *on behalf of* 3. 的 De-phrase with the Head Noun Omitted 4. 太 tài…了 le *overly* 5. 能 néng *capability* 6. 多 duō …*and more*
5 Beef Noodles Are Really Delicious	Food and Drink	1. Learning the names of common foods and describing their taste. 2. Learning to express likes for and make simple comments about food. 3. Learning to describe what somebody can/can't do and how well one does it. 4. Learning to ask for help.	1. 有一點 yǒu yìdiǎn *slightly* 2. Complement Marker 得 de 3. Acquired Skills 會 huì 4. Destination Marker 到 dào

Bits of Chinese Culture	Notes on Pinyin and Pronunciation	Introduction to Chinese Characters
1. Tea Culture 2. Chinese Nicknames	1. The Tones 2. Third Tone Change 3. Bù (不) Tone Changes	Basic Chinese Strokes
Family Central to Chinese Culture	1. Pinyin Rules (1) 2. Tone Changes for 一 Yī	1. Basic Structure of Chinese Characters 2. Basic Template for Chinese Calligraphy
A One-of-a-kind Leisure Activity — Shrimp Fishing	Pinyin Rules (2)	Using Components to Learn Chinese Characters
Around-the-clock Convenience Stores	1. Pinyin Rules (3) 2. Tone Mark Rules (Position of the Tone Marks)	Basic Chinese Radicals
1. Queuing up at Food Stands 2. Street Vendors in Taiwan	Pinyin Rules (4)	The Earliest Chinese Characters

詞類表　Parts of Speech in Chinese

List of Parts of Speech in Chinese

Symbols	Parts of speech	八大詞類	Examples
N	noun	名詞	水、五、昨天、學校、他、幾
V	verb	動詞	吃、告訴、容易、快樂、知道、破
Adv	adverb	副詞	很、不、常、到處、也、就、難道
Conj	conjunction	連詞	和、跟、而且、雖然、因為
Prep	preposition	介詞	從、對、向、跟、在、給
M	measure	量詞	個、張、碗、次、頓、公尺
Ptc	particle	助詞	的、得、啊、嗎、完、掉、把、喂
Det	determiner	限定詞	這、那、某、每、哪

Verb Classification

Symbols	Classification	動詞分類	Examples
V	transitive action verbs	及物動作動詞	買、做、說
Vi	intransitive action verbs	不及物動作動詞	跑、坐、睡、笑
V-sep	intransitive action verbs, separable	不及物動作離合詞	唱歌、上網、打架
Vs	intransitive state verbs	不及物狀態動詞	冷、高、漂亮
Vst	transitive state verbs	及物狀態動詞	關心、喜歡、同意
Vs-attr	intransitive state verbs, attributive only	唯定不及物狀態動詞	野生、公共、新興
Vs-pred	intransitive state verbs, predicative only	唯謂不及物狀態動詞	夠、多、少
Vs-sep	intransitive state verbs, separable	不及物狀態離合詞	放心、幽默、生氣
Vaux	auxiliary verbs	助動詞	會、能、可以
Vp	intransitive process verbs	不及物變化動詞	破、感冒、壞、死
Vpt	transitive process verbs	及物變化動詞	忘記、變成、丟
Vp-sep	intransitive process verbs, separable	不及物變化離合詞	結婚、生病、畢業

Default Values of the Symbols

Symbols	Default values
V	action, transitive
Vs	state, intransitive
Vp	process, intransitive
V-sep	separable, intransitive

課堂用語 Classroom Phrases

1 上課了。
Shàngkè le.
Let's begin the class.

2 請打開書。
Qǐng dǎkāi shū.
Open your book.

3 請看第五頁。
Qǐng kàn dì wǔ yè.
Please see page 5.

4 我說，你們聽。
Wǒ shuō, nǐmen tīng.
I'll speak, you listen.

5 請跟我說。
Qǐng gēn wǒ shuō.
Please repeat after me.

6 請再說 / 念一次。
Qǐng zài shuō/niàn yí cì.
Please say it again.

7 請回答。
Qǐng huídá.
Please answer my question.

8 請問，這個字怎麼念 / 寫？
Qǐngwèn, zhè ge zì zěnme niàn/xiě?
How do you pronounce/spell this word?

9 對了！
Duì le!
Right! Correct!

10 不對。
Bú duì.
Wrong. Incorrect.

11 請念對話。
Qǐng niàn duìhuà.
Read the dialogue, please.

12 請看黑板。
Qǐng kàn hēibǎn.
Look at the board, please.

13 懂不懂？
Dǒng bù dǒng?
Do you understand?

14 懂了！
Dǒng le!
Yes, I/we understand.

15 有沒有問題？
Yǒu méi yǒu wèntí?
Any question?

16 很好！
Hěn hǎo!
Very good!

17 下課。
Xiàkè.
The class is over.

人物介紹　**Introduction to Characters**

李明華

Lǐ Mínghuá

Li Ming-hua is from Taipei, Taiwan.
Male. Age 32. Single.

He works in a bank. He has worked in Vietnam for 6 months and is an acquaintance of Yue-mei Chen's father, who entrusted the responsibility of taking care of his daughter to Ming-hua. They met at the airport.

陳月美

Chén Yuèměi

Chen Yue-mei is from Hanoi, Vietnam.
Female. Age 22.

She traveled to Taiwan with her father's friend, Wang Kai-wen. They were picked up at the airport by Ming-hua, her father's Taiwanese acquaintance.
She is a student. Ru-yu and An-tong are her classmates.

白如玉

Bái Rúyù

Bai Ru-yu is from New York, USA.
Female. Age 21.

She is a student. Yue-mei and An-tong are her classmates.

馬安同

Mǎ Āntóng

Ma An-tong is from Tegucigalpa, Republic of Honduras.
Male. Age 22.

He is a student. Yue-mei and Ru-yu are his classmates.
He is Yi-jun's language exchange partner and Yi-jun is his best friend in Taiwan.

張怡君

Zhāng Yíjūn

Zhang Yi-jun is a Taiwanese college student.
Female. Age 20.

Her college is situated in a mountain in Hualien. She met An-tong on a trip. She is a language exchange partner of An-tong.

田中誠一

Tiánzhōng Chéngyī

Tianzhong Chengyi is from Tokyo, Japan.
Male. Age 30. Single.

He works in Taiwan as an expatriate of a Japanese motor company. Besides working, he is also learning Chinese in a language center. He is in the same class with Yue-mei, Ru-yu, and An-tong and he happens to be Li Ming-hua's client. Tianzhong's girlfriend is coming to Taiwan and he wants to show her around.

目 次 Contents

序 .... Foreword IV

主編的話 .... From the Editor's Desk VI

系列規畫 .... About the Series VII

改版緣起 .... Reasons for the Revision VIII

AR 使用步驟 .... How to Use AR IX

漢語介紹 .... An Introduction to the Chinese Language X

各課重點 .... Highlights of Lessons XX

詞 類 表 .... Parts of Speech in Chinese XXII

課堂用語 .... Classroom Phrases XXIII

人物介紹 .... Introduction to Characters XXIV

Contents

第一課 Lesson 1 歡迎你來臺灣！ 1
Welcome to Taiwan!

第二課 Lesson 2 我的家人 23
My Family

第三課 Lesson 3 週末做什麼？ 43
What Are You Doing Over the Weekend?

第四課 Lesson 4 請問一共多少錢？ 65
Excuse Me. How Much Does That Cost in Total?

第五課 Lesson 5 牛肉麵真好吃 85
Beef Noodles Are Really Delicious

Appendix

I. 生詞索引 I （中－英）Vocabulary Index (Chinese-English) 103

II. 生詞索引 II （英－中）Vocabulary Index (English-Chinese) 111

III. 簡體字課文參考 Text in Simplified Characters 120

LESSON 1

第一課

歡迎你來臺灣！
Welcome to Taiwan!

學習目標 Learning Objectives

Topic: 自我介紹 Introducing Myself

- Learning simple greetings.
- Learning simple phrases to introduce people.
- Learning simple phrases to discuss likes/dislikes.
- Learning simple phrases to express gratitude.

歡迎你來臺灣！

Welcome to Taiwan!

對話一 Dialogue 1 01-01 01-A

明 華	：	請問 你 是 陳月美 小姐 嗎？
Mínghuá	：	Qǐngwèn nǐ shì Chén Yuèměi xiǎojiě ma?
月 美	：	是的。謝謝 你 來 接 我們。
Yuèměi	：	Shìde. Xièxie nǐ lái jiē wǒmen.
明 華	：	不客氣。我 是 李明華。
Mínghuá	：	Búkèqì. Wǒ shì Lǐ Mínghuá.
月 美	：	這 是 王先生。
Yuèměi	：	Zhè shì Wáng Xiānshēng.
開 文	：	你好。我 姓 王，叫 開文。
Kāiwén	：	Nǐ hǎo. Wǒ xìng Wáng, jiào Kāiwén.
明 華	：	你們 好。歡迎 你們 來 臺灣。
Mínghuá	：	Nǐmen hǎo. Huānyíng nǐmen lái Táiwān.

課文英譯 Text in English

Minghua : Excuse me, are you Miss Chen Yuemei?
Yuemei : Yes. Thank you for coming to pick us up.
Minghua : You're welcome. My name is Minghua Li.
Yuemei : This is Mr. Wang.
Kaiwen : Hi, my surname is Wang. My first name is Kaiwen.
Minghua : How are you? Welcome to Taiwan.

生詞一 Vocabulary 01-02

People in the dialogue

1	陳月美	Chén Yuèměi	ㄔㄣˊ ㄩㄝˋ ㄇㄟˇ		a woman from Vietnam
2	李明華	Lǐ Mínghuá	ㄌㄧˇ ㄇㄧㄥˊ ㄏㄨㄚˊ		a man from Taiwan
3	王開文	Wáng Kāiwén	ㄨㄤˊ ㄎㄞ ㄨㄣˊ		a man from the US

Vocabulary

4	你	nǐ	ㄋㄧˇ	(N)	you
5	來	lái	ㄌㄞˊ	(V)	to come
6	是	shì	ㄕˋ	(Vst)	to be
7	小姐	xiǎojiě	ㄒㄧㄠˇ ㄐㄧㄝˇ	(N)	Miss, Ms.
8	嗎	ma	˙ㄇㄚ	(Ptc)	sentence final particle
9	接	jiē	ㄐㄧㄝ	(V)	to pick sb up
10	我們	wǒmen	ㄨㄛˇ ˙ㄇㄣ	(N)	we, us
11	我	wǒ	ㄨㄛˇ	(N)	I, me
12	這	zhè / zhèi	ㄓㄜˋ/ㄓㄟˋ	(Det)	this
13	先生	xiānshēng	ㄒㄧㄢ ㄕㄥ	(N)	Mr.
14	好	hǎo	ㄏㄠˇ	(Vs)	fine, well
15	姓	xìng	ㄒㄧㄥˋ	(Vst)	to be surnamed
16	叫	jiào	ㄐㄧㄠˋ	(Vst)	to be called, i.e., to have the first name xx
17	你們	nǐmen	ㄋㄧˇ ˙ㄇㄣ	(N)	you (plural)

Names

18	臺灣 （＝台灣）	Táiwān	ㄊㄞˊ ㄨㄢ	Taiwan

Phrases

19	歡迎	huānyíng	ㄏㄨㄢ ㄧㄥˊ	welcome
20	請問	qǐngwèn	ㄑㄧㄥˇ ㄨㄣˋ	May I ask you... Excuse me,...
21	是的	shìde	ㄕˋ ㄉㄜ˙	yes
22	謝謝	xièxie	ㄒㄧㄝˋ ㄒㄧㄝ˙	Thank you.
23	不客氣	búkèqì	ㄅㄨˊ ㄎㄜˋ ㄑㄧˋ	You're welcome.
24	你好	nǐ hǎo	ㄋㄧˇ ㄏㄠˇ	How are you? Hello.

對話二 Dialogue 2　🎧 01-03　 01-B

明　　華　：請 喝 茶。
Mínghuá　：Qǐng hē chá.

開　　文　：謝謝。很 好喝。請問 這是 什麼 茶？
Kāiwén　：Xièxie. Hěn hǎohē. Qǐngwèn zhè shì shénme chá?

明　　華　：這是 烏龍茶。臺灣 人 喜歡 喝 茶。
Mínghuá　：Zhè shì Wūlóng chá. Táiwān rén xǐhuān hē chá.
　　　　　開文，你們 日本人 呢？
　　　　　Kāiwén, nǐmen Rìběn rén ne?

月　　美　：他 不 是 日本人。
Yuèměi　：Tā bú shì Rìběn rén.

明　　華　：對不起，你 是 哪 國 人？
Mínghuá　：Duìbùqǐ, nǐ shì nǎ guó rén?

開　　文　：我 是 美國人。
Kāiwén　：Wǒ shì Měiguó rén.

明　　華　：開文，你 要 不 要 喝 咖啡？
Mínghuá　：Kāiwén, nǐ yào bú yào hē kāfēi?

開　　文　：謝謝！我 不 喝 咖啡，我 喜歡 喝 茶。
Kāiwén　：Xièxie! Wǒ bù hē kāfēi, wǒ xǐhuān hē chá.

課文英譯 Text in English

Minghua　：Please have some tea.

Kaiwen　：Thank you. This tastes good. May I ask what kind of tea this is?

Minghua　：This is Oolong tea. Taiwanese like to drink tea. Kaiwen, how about you Japanese people?

Yuemei　：He is not Japanese.

Minghua　：I am sorry. Which country are you from?

Kaiwen　：I am American.

Minghua　：Kaiwen, would you like to drink coffee?

Kaiwen　：Thank you. I don't drink coffee. I like to drink tea.

生詞二 Vocabulary 2 01-04

Vocabulary

1	請	qǐng	ㄑㄧㄥˇ	(V)	please
2	喝	hē	ㄏㄜ	(V)	to drink
3	茶	chá	ㄔㄚˊ	(N)	tea
4	很	hěn	ㄏㄣˇ	(Adv)	very
5	好喝	hǎohē	ㄏㄠˇ ㄏㄜ	(Vs)	(lit. good to drink) to taste good
6	什麼	shénme	ㄕㄣˊ ㄇㄜ˙	(N)	what
7	人	rén	ㄖㄣˊ	(N)	person, people
8	喜歡	xǐhuān	ㄒㄧˇ ㄏㄨㄢ	(Vst)	to like
9	呢	ne	ㄋㄜ˙	(Ptc)	sentence final particle
10	他	tā	ㄊㄚ	(N)	he, him
11	不	bù	ㄅㄨˋ	(Adv)	not
12	哪	nǎ / něi	ㄋㄚˇ / ㄋㄟˇ	(Det)	which
13	要	yào	ㄧㄠˋ	(Vaux)	to want to
14	咖啡	kāfēi	ㄎㄚ ㄈㄟ	(N)	coffee

Names

15	烏龍茶	Wūlóng chá	ㄨ ㄌㄨㄥˊ ㄔㄚˊ		Oolong tea
16	日本	Rìběn	ㄖˋ ㄅㄣˇ		Japan
17	美國	Měiguó	ㄇㄟˇ ㄍㄨㄛˊ		America

Phrases

18	對不起	duìbùqǐ	ㄉㄨㄟˋ ㄅㄨˋ ㄑㄧˇ		I'm sorry.
19	哪國	nǎ guó / něi guó	ㄋㄚˇ ㄍㄨㄛˊ / ㄋㄟˇ ㄍㄨㄛˊ		Which country?

文法 Grammar

I. Ways to Ask Questions in Chinese 🎧 01-05

A. Asking Questions with A-not-A

Function: The A-not-A form of making a question is the most neutral way to ask a question in Chinese and closest to yes/no questions in English.

1 王先生要不要喝咖啡？

Wáng Xiānshēng yào bú yào hē kāfēi?

Does Mr. Wang want to have some coffee?

2 這是不是烏龍茶？

Zhè shì bú shì Wūlóng chá?

Is this Oolong tea?

3 臺灣人喜歡不喜歡喝茶？

Táiwān rén xǐhuān bù xǐhuān hē chá?

Do Taiwanese people like to drink tea?

Structures: The "A" in the structure refers to the first verbal element.

1 他喝咖啡。

Tā hē kāfēi.

He'll have coffee.

他喝不喝咖啡？

Tā hē bù hē kāfēi?

Does he want to drink coffee?

2 你是日本人。

Nǐ shì Rìběn rén.

You are Japanese.

你是不是日本人？

Nǐ shì bú shì Rìběn rén?

Are you Japanese?

3 他來臺灣。

Tā lái Táiwān.

He came to Taiwan.

他來不來臺灣？

Tā lái bù lái Táiwān?

Is he coming to Taiwan?

Usage: When the verbal element in an A-not-A question is disyllabic (XY), the second syllable (Y) can be dropped in the first "A" of the pattern, so "XY-not-XY" is the same as "X-not-XY". For example, 你喜歡不喜歡我？Nǐ xǐhuān bù xǐhuān wǒ? is the same as 你喜不喜歡我？Nǐ xǐ bù xǐhuān wǒ? (Do you like me?)

練習 Exercise

Complete questions using A-not-A form.

1 李明華 _____ 不 _____ 美國人？
李明華是美國人。

2 陳月美 _____ 不 _____ 臺灣？
陳月美來臺灣。

3 王先生 _____ 不 _____ 喝咖啡？
王先生喜歡喝咖啡。

4 他 _____ 不 _____ 喝茶？
他不要喝茶。

5 他 _____ 不 _____ 來臺北？
他要來臺北（Táiběi, Taipei）。

B. Asking Questions with 嗎 ma 🎧 01-06

Function: Questions can be formed using the question particle 嗎 *ma*. It is usually used for short questions.

1 你好嗎？
Nǐ hǎo ma?
How are you?

2 你來接我們嗎？
Nǐ lái jiē wǒmen ma?
Are you here to pick us up?

3 他是日本人嗎？
Tā shì Rìběn rén ma?
Is he Japanese?

8

Structures: SENTENCE + 嗎 *ma*? The sentence in 嗎 *ma* questions can be either in the affirmative or negative.

✏️ Negation:

① 他不姓陳嗎？
Tā bú xìng Chén ma?
Isn't he surnamed Chen?

② 你不是臺灣人嗎？
Nǐ bú shì Táiwān rén ma?
Aren't you Taiwanese?

③ 他不喝咖啡嗎？
Tā bù hē kāfēi ma?
Doesn't he drink coffee?

Usage: The A-not-A question form indicates no assumption, and is used for neutral inquiries or longer inquiries. It does not take a 嗎 *ma* question particle at the end of the sentence. One cannot say *這是不是茶嗎？ Zhè shì bú shì chá ma? ('Is this tea?'). 嗎 *ma* questions, by contrast, are used for short inquiries. But in most cases, these two forms of question are often interchangeable.

① 你好嗎？
Nǐ hǎo ma?
How are you?

② 你要喝茶嗎？
Nǐ yào hē chá ma?
Do you want to drink tea?

③ 你們要不要喝烏龍茶？
Nǐmen yào bú yào hē Wūlóng chá?
Do you want to drink Oolong tea?

練習 Exercise

Complete questions using 嗎 *ma* based on the responses to the right.

Question	Response
① _____	？ 他叫明華。
② _____	？ 陳小姐是臺灣人。
③ _____	？ 他喜歡喝咖啡。

④ _____？ 王先生叫開文。

⑤ _____？ 他不是日本人。

II. Answering Questions in Chinese 🎧 01-07

A. Affirmative Answers

Affirmative answers can be formed by repeating the main verb in the question, followed by a sentence in the affirmative, e.g.,

❶ A：他是不是臺灣人？／他是臺灣人嗎？

Tā shì bú shì Táiwān rén? / Tā shì Táiwān rén ma?

Is he Taiwanese?

B：是，他是臺灣人。

Shì, tā shì Táiwān rén.

Yes, he is Taiwanese.

❷ A：你喜不喜歡臺灣？／你喜歡臺灣嗎？

Nǐ xǐ bù xǐhuān Táiwān? / Nǐ xǐhuān Táiwān ma?

Do you like Taiwan?

B：喜歡，我喜歡臺灣。

Xǐhuān, wǒ xǐhuān Táiwān.

Yes, I like Taiwan.

❸ A：王先生是不是日本人？／王先生是日本人嗎？

Wáng Xiānshēng shì bú shì Rìběn rén? /

Wáng Xiānshēng shì Rìběn rén ma?

Is Mr. Wang Japanese ?

B：是，王先生是日本人。

Shì, Wáng Xiānshēng shì Rìběn rén.

Yes, Mr. Wang is Japanese.

❹ A：他喝不喝烏龍茶？／他喝烏龍茶嗎？

Tā hē bù hē Wūlóng chá? / Tā hē Wūlóng chá ma?

Does he drink Oolong tea?

B：喝，他喝烏龍茶。

Hē, tā hē Wūlóng chá.

Yes, he drinks Oolong tea.

In Chinese, short answers in the affirmative can be made by simply repeating the verb from the question.

1 你是王先生嗎？　　　　　　　是。

Nǐ shì Wáng Xiānshēng ma?　　Shì.

Are you Mr. Wang?　　　　　　Yes.

2 他來不來臺灣？　　　　　　　來。

Tā lái bù lái Táiwān?　　　　　Lái.

Will he come to Taiwan?　　　　Yes.

3 他喜歡不喜歡喝茶？　　　　　喜歡。

Tā xǐhuān bù xǐhuān hē chá?　　Xǐhuān.

Does he like tea?　　　　　　　Yes.

練習 Exercise

Give affirmative responses.

Question	Response
1 臺灣人喜歡不喜歡喝茶？	_____
2 你要不要喝咖啡？	_____
3 你喜歡他嗎？	_____
4 他是不是日本人？	_____
5 你要喝烏龍茶嗎？	_____

B. Negative Replies with 不 bù 01-08

Negative replies can be formed by repeating the main verb in its negative form, i.e., 不 *bù* + verb, followed by a sentence in the negative. 不 *bù* is an adverb which is placed before a verb or another adverb, e.g.,

1 他是不是李先生？

Tā shì bú shì Lǐ Xiānshēng?

Is he Mr. Li?

不是，他不是李先生。

Bú shì, tā bú shì Lǐ Xiānshēng.

No, he is not Mr. Li.

2 王先生喝茶嗎？

Wáng Xiānshēng hē chá ma?

Does Mr. Wang drink tea?

不，他不喝。

Bù, tā bù hē.

No, he doesn't drink tea.

3 李小姐是不是臺灣人？

Lǐ Xiǎojiě shì bú shì Táiwān rén?

Is Miss Li Taiwanese?

不是，李小姐不是臺灣人。

Bú shì, Lǐ Xiǎojiě bú shì Táiwān rén.

No, Miss Li is not Taiwanese.

In Chinese, the answer to a question can consist of just the verb in the question asked.

1 他要不要喝咖啡？

Tā yào bú yào hē kāfēi?

Does he want to drink coffee?

不要。

Bú yào.

No.

2 你喜歡不喜歡喝烏龍茶？

Nǐ xǐhuān bù xǐhuān hē Wūlóng chá?

Do you like to drink Oolong tea?

不喜歡。

Bù xǐhuān.

No.

3 陳小姐是不是美國人？

Chén Xiǎojiě shì bú shì Měiguó rén?

Is Miss Chen American?

不是。

Bú shì.

No.

Usage: There are some exceptions to the rules above. For example, when the verb is 姓 *xìng* "to be surnamed" or 叫 *jiào* "to be called". When the question is 他姓李嗎？ Tā xìng Lǐ ma? 'Is he surnamed Li?', the negative reply should be 不姓李 Bú xìng Lǐ '(He is) not surnamed Li.', rather than *不姓 *bú xìng*. When the question is 李先生叫開文嗎？ Lǐ Xiānshēng jiào Kāiwén ma? 'Is Mr. Li called Kaiwen?', the negative reply should be 不叫開文 Bú jiào Kāiwén '(He is) not called Kaiwen.', rather than *不叫 *bú jiào*.

練習 Exercise

Please answer the questions based on the pictures given below.

❶ 李小姐是美國人嗎？

❷ 他是陳先生嗎？

❸ 他喜歡喝茶嗎？

❹ 王小姐要不要喝咖啡？

❺ 他叫明華嗎？

III. Modification Marker 很 hěn   01-09

Function: The adverb 很 *hěn* modifies state verbs (Vs).

❶ 我很好。
Wǒ hěn hǎo.
I am fine.

❷ 他很喜歡臺灣。
Tā hěn xǐhuān Táiwān.
He likes Taiwan.

❸ 臺灣人很喜歡喝烏龍茶。
Táiwān rén hěn xǐhuān hē Wūlóng chá.
Taiwanese people like to drink Oolong tea.

Structures: The adverb 很 *hěn* is placed before state verbs (Vs) as follows: Subject 很 *hěn* + State Verb.

1 烏龍茶很好喝。

Wūlóng chá hěn hǎohē.

Oolong tea tastes good.

2 他很喜歡日本人。

Tā hěn xǐhuān Rìběn rén.

He likes Japanese people.

3 我們很好。

Wǒmen hěn hǎo.

We are fine.

Usage: In general, adjectival state verbs must be preceded by either 不 or intensifiers. When no particular intensity is intended, they are preceded by 很 *hěn*. That is, 很 *hěn* + stative verb means 'very stative verb' (very expensive, very good, very tall, etc.) and sometimes it just means a stative verb. When 很 is intended to actually mean 'very', it is typically stressed in speech.

練習 Exercise

(1-2 not stressed, 3-5 stressed)

1 你好嗎？　　　　　　　　我很好。

2 李明華喜歡他嗎？　　　　李明華很喜歡他。

3 陳小姐不喜歡喝茶嗎？　　陳小姐**很**喜歡喝茶。

Yes, she **does**.

4 王先生不喜歡臺灣嗎？　　他**很**喜歡臺灣。

Yes, he **does**.

5 明華不喜歡月美嗎？　　　他**很**喜歡。

Yes, he (actually) **does**.

IV. Contrastive Questions with 呢 ne 01-10

Function: The 呢 *ne* question is a tag question with a short form following a statement.

1 我要喝茶，你呢？
Wǒ yào hē chá, nǐ ne?
I want to drink tea, and you?

2 他不喝咖啡，陳小姐呢？
Tā bù hē kāfēi, Chén Xiǎojiě ne?
He does not drink coffee. What about Miss Chen?

3 王先生是日本人，李先生呢？
Wáng Xiānshēng shì Rìběn rén, Lǐ Xiānshēng ne?
Mr. Wang is Japanese. What about Mr. Li?

Structures:

1. Same predicate, different subjects
   S1 V O, S2 呢 *ne*?

   (1) 他是美國人，你呢？
   Tā shì Měiguó rén, nǐ ne?
   He's American. And you?

   (2) 他喜歡我們，你呢？
   Tā xǐhuān wǒmen, nǐ ne?
   He likes us. How about you?

2. Same subject, different predicates
   S V O1, O2 呢 *ne*?

   (1) 你喜歡喝茶，咖啡呢？
   Nǐ xǐhuān hē chá, kāfēi ne?
   You like to drink tea. How about coffee?

   (2) 他不喝咖啡，茶呢？
   Tā bù hē kāfēi, chá ne?
   He doesn't drink coffee. How about tea?

練習 Exercise

1-3 same predicate, different subjects. 4-5 same subject, different predicates.

1 陳小姐來臺北，王先生呢？

2 日本人喜歡喝咖啡，＿＿＿＿＿＿＿＿＿＿＿＿＿＿＿ 呢？

3 他來臺灣，李先生呢？

4 你不喝咖啡，＿＿＿＿＿＿＿＿＿＿＿＿＿＿＿＿ ？

5 他喝烏龍茶，＿＿＿＿＿＿＿＿＿＿＿＿＿ ？

課 室 活 動 Classroom Activities

I. Introducing Yourself and Others

Goal: Learning to give and obtain basic personal information.

Task: Pair up with a classmate, say hello, and introduce yourself. Then ask him/her for his/her name, where s/he is from, and introduce him/her to the class.

你好，我姓王，叫開文，我是美國人。你呢？

我叫國生美月，我是日本人。

II. Likes and Dislikes

Goal: Learning to ask whether someone likes to drink tea or coffee.

Task: Use the A-not-A form 喜歡不喜歡 to ask a classmate whether s/he likes to drink tea/coffee. If the answer is in the affirmative, then treat him/her to one. If the answer is in the negative, give other options.

喝茶

喝咖啡

III. Expressing Thanks

Goal: Learning to respond to inquiries and express thanks.

Task: Pair up for a conversation. Ask questions like:

A：你要不要…？

Nǐ yào bú yào...?

Would you like...?

B：好的 / 不要，謝謝。

Hǎode / Bú yào, xièxie.

Yes / No, thank you.

IV. Obtaining Information

Goal: Learning to use 呢 *ne* questions to obtain more information.

Task: Make sentences based on the pictures below. Then use a " 呢 question" to ask your classmate for information. E.g.,

A：陳月美喜歡…。王開文呢？

B：他不喜歡…，他喜歡…。

文化 *Bits of Chinese Culture*

Tea Culture

"Come over for some tea!" is a common phrase used much like the phrase in English, "You really have to drop by my place sometime for a cup of coffee". In Taiwan, friends gather around a table with a tea set on it in their free time and drink tea. They drink the tea from delicate, little teacups and might discuss its fragrance and taste. Chatting over tea is a favorite way of the Chinese to bond and keep abreast of the latest things in their lives.

▲ Chinese tea making
資深茶人黃浩然 示範
《台灣喫茶》吳德亮 / 著作、攝影

At home, many people make themselves a cup of hot tea or prepare a pot for the family for after-dinner conversation. Many people like to start off the day at the office with a cup of tea. Those with a more discerning palate might make tea using tea leaves, while teabags probably suffices for others. In the end, they all enjoy a nice cup of hot tea.

In the shade of old trees in parks or near temples, you can find folks sitting around small tables drinking tea and snacking on melon seeds. Tea is an everyday part of life of the people of Taiwan.

▲ Tea sets
《台灣喫茶》吳德亮 / 著作、攝影

▲ A tea house in Taiwan
《台灣喫茶》吳德亮 / 著作、攝影

Chinese Nicknames

It is customary for Chinese to call friends and loved ones by nicknames. The character " 老 " *lǎo* is sometimes added before the last name or " 小 " *xiǎo* placed in front of the second character of the given name to form nicknames. Due to the influence of the Taiwanese dialect, nicknames in Taiwan are often formed by placing the character " 阿 " *ā* in front of the name or the second character of the given name is repeated. For example, someone by the name of " 陳文華 " could be nicknamed " 老陳 ," " 小陳 ," " 小華 ," " 華華 ," or " 阿華 ."

Notes on Pinyin and Pronunciation

1. The Tones 基本聲調

First tone	一聲（一）	接 jiē、喝 hē、他 tā
Second tone	二聲（ˊ）	來 lái、茶 chá、人 rén
Third tone	三聲（ˇ）	你 nǐ、我 wǒ、請 qǐng、很 hěn、哪 nǎ
Fourth tone	四聲（ˋ）	是 shì、這 zhè、姓 xìng、叫 jiào、要 yào
Neutral tone (no tone mark)	輕聲	嗎 ma、呢 ne ／我們 wǒmen、你們 nǐmen、是的 shìde、謝謝 xièxie、什麼 shénme

2. Third Tone Change 三聲變調

(1) When two characters with third tones are found together, the first third tone is pronounced with a second tone as in these two examples in this lesson:

小姐 xiǎojiě（ˇ+ˇ→ˊ ˇ）　你好 nǐ hǎo（ˇ+ˇ→ˊ ˇ）

Despite the change in pronunciation, however, it is still marked as a third tone in pinyin.

(2) Rules for third-tone changes 三聲變調原則：

ˇ ˇ (ˊ) 小 姐	ˇ　ˇ ˇ 　(ˊ) 我　很 好	ˇ　ˇ (ˊ)　ˉ 很 　好喝
ˇ ˇ (ˊ) 你 好	ˇ　ˇ ˇ 　(ˊ) 李　小 姐	ˇ　ˇ ˉ (ˊ) 我　喜歡
ˇ ˇ (ˊ) 很 好		ˇ　ˇ (ˊ) 你　好嗎

3. Bù (不) Tone changes「不」的變調

The tone for 不 *bù* changes depending on the tone of the character that follows it. When 不 *bù* is followed by a character with a first, second, or third tone, 不 *bù* is pronounced and the pinyin marked with a fourth tone （ˋ）. When 不 *bù* is followed by a character with a fourth tone, it is pronounced and the pinyin marked with a second tone （ˊ）.

不 bù + character with 1st, 2nd or 3rd tone → 不 pronounced with 4th tone (4th tone mark)		不 bù + character with 4th tone → 不 pronounced with 2nd tone (2nd tone mark)	
	ˋ 不	一 喝咖啡	ˊ 不	ˋ 客氣
(來)	ˋ 不	ˊ 來	ˊ 不	ˋ 是
(對)	ˋ 不	ˇ 喜歡 起	(要) ˊ 不	ˋ 要

Introduction to Chinese Characters

Basic Chinese Strokes

Chinese calligraphy consists of eight basic strokes. These are also the basic strokes of Chinese characters. These eight basic strokes are "horizontal"（橫 héng）, "vertical"（豎 shù）, "brush left"（撇 piě）, "press down and drag"（捺 nà）, "dot"（點 diǎn）, "flick"（挑 tiǎo）, "hook"（鈎 gōu）, and "corner fold"（折 zhé）. They are used to teach beginners to write Chinese characters.

Basic Strokes	一	丨	ノ	㇏	丶	ノ	亅	㇆
Stroke name in Chinese (pinyin)	橫 ㄏㄥˊ héng	豎 ㄕㄨˋ shù	撇 ㄆㄧㄝˇ piě	捺 ㄋㄚˋ nà	點 ㄉㄧㄢˇ diǎn	挑 ㄊㄧㄠˇ tiǎo	鈎 ㄍㄡ gōu	折 ㄓㄜˊ zhé
Direction of stroke	→	↓	↙	↘	↘	↗	↓	⌐→↓
Example	不	叫	你	人	文	接	小	日

Self-Assessment Checklist

I can use greetings.

20%   40%   60%   80%   100%

I can use simple phrases to introduce people.

20%   40%   60%   80%   100%

I can use simple phrases to discuss likes/dislikes.

20%   40%   60%   80%   100%

I can use simple phrases to express gratitude.

20%   40%   60%   80%   100%

第二課

我的家人
My Family

Topic: 家人 Family Members

- Learning to talk about people in my family members and their names.
- Learning to describe people, places, and possessions.
- Learning to talk about the number of people in a family.

我的家人
My Family

對話一 Dialogue 1 02-01 02-A

怡　　君	：	這是我家。請進！
Yíjūn	：	Zhè shì wǒ jiā. Qǐng jìn!
安　　同	：	很漂亮的房子！
Āntóng	：	Hěn piàoliàng de fángzi!

[They enter Yijun's house.]

怡　　君	：	請坐！要不要喝茶？
Yíjūn	：	Qǐng zuò! Yào bú yào hē chá?
安　　同	：	好，謝謝你。你家有很多照片。
Āntóng	：	Hǎo, xièxie nǐ. Nǐ jiā yǒu hěn duō zhàopiàn.
怡　　君	：	我家人都很喜歡照相。
Yíjūn	：	Wǒ jiārén dōu hěn xǐhuān zhàoxiàng.

安　同　：這張照片很好看。這是誰？你姐姐嗎？
Āntóng　：Zhè zhāng zhàopiàn hěn hǎokàn. Zhè shì shéi? Nǐ jiějie ma?

怡　君　：不是，是我妹妹。這是我爸爸、媽媽。
Yíjūn　：Bú shì, shì wǒ mèimei. Zhè shì wǒ bàba, māma.

安　同　：你家人都很好看。
Āntóng　：Nǐ jiārén dōu hěn hǎokàn.

課文英譯 Text in English

Yijun	: This is my house. Please come in.
Antong	: This is a pretty house.
Yijun	: Please have a seat. Would you like some tea?
Antong	: Yes, thank you. You have a lot of pictures in your house.
Yijun	: The people in my family like to take pictures.
Antong	: This is a nice picture. Who is this? Your older sister?
Yijun	: No, that is my younger sister. These are my dad and mom.
Antong	: The people in your family are very good-looking.

生詞一 Vocabulary 1　🎧 02-02

People in the dialogue

| 1 | 張怡君 | Zhāng Yíjūn | ㄓㄤ ㄧˊ ㄐㄩㄣ | a woman from Taiwan |
| 2 | 馬安同 | Mǎ Āntóng | ㄇㄚˇ ㄢ ㄊㄨㄥˊ | a man from the Republic of Honduras |

Vocabulary

3	的	de	ㄉㄜ˙	(Ptc)	modification marker
4	家人	jiārén	ㄐㄚ ㄖㄣˊ	(N)	family (members)
5	家	jiā	ㄐㄚ	(N)	home, house
6	漂亮	piàoliàng	ㄆㄧㄠˋ ㄌㄧㄤˋ	(Vs)	pretty

7	房子	fángzi	ㄈㄤˊ ㄗ˙	(N)	house
8	坐	zuò	ㄗㄨㄛˋ	(Vi)	to sit
9	好	hǎo	ㄏㄠˇ	(Ptc)	OK
10	有	yǒu	ㄧㄡˇ	(Vst)	to have
11	多	duō	ㄉㄨㄛ	(Vs-pred)	many
12	照片	zhàopiàn	ㄓㄠˋ ㄆㄧㄢˋ	(N)	photo
13	都	dōu	ㄉㄡ	(Adv)	all, both
14	照相	zhàoxiàng	ㄓㄠˋ ㄒㄧㄤˋ	(V-sep)	to take a photo
15	張	zhāng	ㄓㄤ	(M)	measure word for flat objects (e.g., paper, tickets)
16	好看	hǎokàn	ㄏㄠˇ ㄎㄢˋ	(Vs)	good-looking
17	誰	shéi	ㄕㄟˊ	(N)	who
18	姐姐	jiějie	ㄐㄧㄝˇ ㄐㄧㄝ˙	(N)	older sister
19	妹妹	mèimei	ㄇㄟˋ ㄇㄟ˙	(N)	younger sister
20	爸爸	bàba	ㄅㄚˋ ㄅㄚ˙	(N)	dad
21	媽媽	māma	ㄇㄚ ㄇㄚ˙	(N)	mom

Phrases

| 22 | 請進 | qǐng jìn | ㄑㄧㄥˇ ㄐㄧㄣˋ | | Please come in! |

對話二 Dialogue 2 🎧 02-03 AR 02-B

明華 Mínghuá	:	田中，歡迎！歡迎！請進。 Tiánzhōng, huānyíng! Huānyíng! Qǐng jìn.
田中 Tiánzhōng	:	謝謝。 Xièxie.
明華 Mínghuá	:	田中，這是我媽媽。 Tiánzhōng, zhè shì wǒ māma.
田中 Tiánzhōng	:	伯母，您好。 Bómǔ, nín hǎo.
明華的媽媽 Mínghuá de māma	:	你好，你好。來！來！來！請坐。 你叫什麼名字？ Nǐ hǎo, nǐ hǎo. Lái! Lái! Lái! Qǐng zuò. Nǐ jiào shénme míngzi?
田中 Tiánzhōng	:	我叫誠一。你們家有很多書。 Wǒ jiào Chéngyī. Nǐmen jiā yǒu hěn duō shū.
明華 Mínghuá	:	都是我哥哥的書。 他是老師，他很喜歡看書。 Dōu shì wǒ gēge de shū. Tā shì lǎoshī, tā hěn xǐhuān kànshū.
明華的媽媽 Mínghuá de māma	:	誠一，你家有幾個人？你有沒有兄弟姐妹？ Chéngyī, nǐ jiā yǒu jǐ ge rén? Nǐ yǒu méi yǒu xiōngdì jiěmèi?
田中 Tiánzhōng	:	我家有五個人，我有兩個妹妹。 Wǒ jiā yǒu wǔ ge rén, wǒ yǒu liǎng ge mèimei.

课文英譯 Text in English

Minghua	:	Tianzhong, welcome, welcome. Please come in.
Tianzhong	:	Thank you!
Minghua	:	Tianzhong, this is my mom.
Tianzhong	:	Mrs. Li (Lit. "Auntie"), how are you?

Minghua's mother : Hello. Come in. Come. Please have a seat. What's your name?

Tianzhong : My name is Chengyi. You have a lot of books.

Minghua : They are all my brother's books. He is a teacher. He likes to read.

Minghua's mother : Chengyi, how many people are there in your family? Do you have any brothers or sisters?

Tianzhong : There are five people in my family. I have two younger sisters.

生詞二 Vocabulary 2 02-04

People in the dialogue

1	田中誠一	Tiánzhōng Chéngyī	ㄊㄧㄢˊ ㄓㄨㄥ ㄔㄥˊ ㄧ		a man from Japan

Vocabulary

2	伯母	bómǔ	ㄅㄛˊ ㄇㄨˇ	(N)	aunt; here a polite term for a friend's mother regardless of age
3	您	nín	ㄋㄧㄣˊ	(N)	you (honorific)
4	名字	míngzi	ㄇㄧㄥˊ ㄗ	(N)	name
5	書	shū	ㄕㄨ	(N)	book
6	哥哥	gēge	ㄍㄜ ㄍㄜ	(N)	older brother
7	老師	lǎoshī	ㄌㄠˇ ㄕ	(N)	teacher
8	看書	kànshū	ㄎㄢˋ ㄕㄨ	(V-sep)	to read
9	幾	jǐ	ㄐㄧˇ	(N)	how many
10	個	ge	ㄍㄜˋ	(M)	general measure word
11	沒	méi	ㄇㄟˊ	(Adv)	not
12	兄弟	xiōngdì	ㄒㄩㄥ ㄉㄧˋ	(N)	brothers
13	姐妹	jiěmèi	ㄐㄧㄝˇ ㄇㄟˋ	(N)	sisters
14	五	wǔ	ㄨˇ	(N)	five
15	兩	liǎng	ㄌㄧㄤˇ	(N)	two

文法 Grammar

I. 的 de *possessive* 🎧 02-05

Function: 的 *de* is used to show possession and is placed between the possessor and the object possessed.

1 我的書
wǒ de shū
my book

2 你們的照片
nǐmen de zhàopiàn
your photo

3 李老師的姐姐
Lǐ lǎoshī de jiějie
teacher Li's sister

4 哥哥的老師
gēge de lǎoshī
brother's teacher

5 我媽媽
wǒ māma
my mom

6 我們老師
wǒmen lǎoshī
our teacher

Structures: Notice that 的 *de* is sometimes omitted, e.g., 5 & 6 above.

1. If the relationship between the possessor and the possessed of the two nouns is close, 的 *de* can be omitted, e.g., 我爸爸 *wǒ bàba* 'my dad', 我哥哥 *wǒ gēge* 'my brother', 我家 *wǒ jiā* 'my home'. Furthermore, the possessor has to be a pronoun when 的 *de* is omitted. So, one can say 李先生的爸爸 *Lǐ Xiānshēng de bàba* 'Mr. Li's dad', but not * 李先生爸爸 *Lǐ Xiānshēng bàba* (omitting 的 *de*).

2. If the two nouns in a possessive relationship refer to an individual and his/her affiliated group, the noun referring to the individual usually appears in the plural rather than the singular form. For example, for 'his home', it is 他們家 *tāmen jiā* (their home), 我們日本 *wǒmen rìběn* (our Japan).

練習 Exercise

Fill in the blanks and add 的 where appropriate.

> A. 的　B. 名字　C. 老師　D. 妹妹　E. 你　F. 你們

1 他 ＿＿＿＿＿＿ ＿＿＿＿＿＿ 是馬安同。

2 陳先生 ＿＿＿＿＿＿ ＿＿＿＿＿＿ 姓李。

3 我 ＿＿＿＿＿＿＿＿ 是老師。

4 ＿＿＿＿＿＿＿＿ 爸爸來不來？

5 ＿＿＿＿＿＿＿＿ 家很漂亮嗎？

II. Modifier Marker 的 de 02-06

Function: 的 *de* is used between the modifier and the head noun.

1 漂亮的小姐
piàoliàng de xiǎojiě
pretty young lady

2 好喝的咖啡
hǎohē de kāfēi
tasty coffee

3 很好看的房子
hěn hǎokàn de fángzi
beautiful house

Usage: Notice that 的 *de* can be omitted when the modifier and the head noun are used together frequently. For example, when talking about nationality, one says 哪國人？ *Něi guó rén?* 'person from which country?', rather than *哪國的人 *Něi guó de rén*. One says 臺灣人 *Táiwān rén* 'Taiwanese people' rather than *臺灣的人 *Táiwān de rén*.

練習 Exercise

Make correct sentences by rearranging the order of the characters.

❶ 人　很好看　的
   ①　 ②　 ③

_____ 多不多？

❷ 的　好喝　茶
  ①　 ②　 ③

王老師要 _____。

❸ 好看　照片　的
  ①　 ②　 ③

我沒有很多 _____。

❹ 房子　漂亮　的
  ①　 ②　 ③

我喜歡 _____。

❺ 的　照片　很多　好看
 ①　 ②　 ③　 ④

他有 _____。

III. 有 yǒu *possessive* 🎧 02-07

Function: The verb 有 *yǒu* refers to possession or ownership.

❶ 我有很多照片。
Wǒ yǒu hěn duō zhàopiàn.
I have many photos.

❷ 他們有好喝的茶。
Tāmen yǒu hǎohē de chá.
They have good-tasting tea.

Structures:

✏️ **Negation:** 有 *yǒu* is always negated with 沒 *méi*.

❶ 他沒有房子。
Tā méi yǒu fángzi.
He does not have a house.

❷ 我沒有書。
Wǒ méi yǒu shū.
I don't have a book.

❸ 對不起，我們沒有烏龍茶。
Duìbùqǐ, wǒmen méi yǒu Wūlóng chá.
Sorry, we don't have any Oolong tea.

❹ 我沒有兄弟姐妹。
Wǒ méi yǒu xiōngdì jiěmèi.
I don't have any brothers or sisters.

Questions: The A-not-A form for the verb 有 *yǒu* is 有沒有 *yǒu méi yǒu*.

① 你們有沒有好喝的咖啡？

Nǐmen yǒu méi yǒu hǎohē de kāfēi?

Do you have good-tasting coffee?

② 你們有烏龍茶嗎？

Nǐmen yǒu Wūlóng chá ma?

Do you have Oolong tea?

③ 你有幾張照片？

Nǐ yǒu jǐ zhāng zhàopiàn?

How many photos do you have?

練習 Exercise

Make correct sentences by rearranging the order of the characters.

① 很多　我們　好喝的咖啡　有
　　　① 　　② 　　　③ 　　　④

_____ 。

② 我哥哥　漂亮的照片　有　沒
　　　① 　　　② 　　　③ ④

_____ 。

③ 兄弟姐妹　有　嗎　你
　　　① 　　② ③ ④

_____ ?

IV. 都 dōu *totality*　　🎧 02-08

Function: 都 *dōu* is used to indicate that all items referred to by the subject or object noun have something in common.

① 我們都姓陳。

Wǒmen dōu xìng Chén.

We are all surnamed Chen.

② 他的兄弟姐妹都很好看。

Tā de xiōngdì jiěmèi dōu hěn hǎokàn.

His siblings are all good looking.

③ 這兩個房子都是他的
（房子）。

Zhè liǎng ge fángzi dōu shì tā de (fángzi).

Both of these two houses are his.

Structures: 都 *dōu* is an adverb, which is placed after the noun it relates to and before the main verb phrase, i.e. Noun + 都 *dōu* + VP.

❶ 我們都是美國人。

Wǒmen dōu shì Měiguó rén.

We are all American.

❷ 你爸爸媽媽都要喝咖啡。

Nǐ bàba māma dōu yào hē kāfēi.

Both your dad and mom want to drink coffee.

❸ 李先生、陳小姐都喜歡喝茶。

Lǐ Xiānshēng, Chén Xiǎojiě dōu xǐhuān hē chá.

Mr. Li and Miss Chen both like to drink tea.

 Negation: Noun + 都 *dōu* + 不 *bù* / 沒 *méi* + VP

❶ 我們都不是美國人。

Wǒmen dōu bú shì Měiguó rén.

None of us is American.

❷ 我哥哥、我姐姐都不喜歡照相。

Wǒ gēge, wǒ jiějie dōu bù xǐhuān zhàoxiàng.

Neither my brother nor my sister likes to take photos.

❸ 我們都沒有哥哥。

Wǒmen dōu méi yǒu gēge.

None of us has any older brother.

Questions:

❶ 你們都是美國人嗎？

Nǐmen dōu shì Měiguó rén ma?

Are you all American?

❷ 你的家人都要喝咖啡嗎？

Nǐ de jiārén dōu yào hē kāfēi ma?

Do all the people in your family want to drink coffee?

Usage:

1. 都 *dōu* is an adverb and appears before the verb and after the subject. It is not correct to say *都我們是臺灣人 Dōu wǒmen shì Táiwān rén.

2. Members of a group indicated by 都 *dōu* all have to appear before 都 *dōu*. For example, to say 'I like both teachers Li and Wang', one says 李老師、王老師，我都喜歡。Lǐ Lǎoshī, Wáng Lǎoshī, wǒ dōu xǐhuān. It is incorrect to say *我都喜歡李老師、王老師。 Wǒ dōu xǐhuān Lǐ Lǎoshī, Wáng Lǎoshī.

3. In interrogatives, 都 *dōu* works with the 嗎 *ma* question form but not with A-not-A question forms. For example, to say 'Are you all surnamed Wang?', one can say 你們都姓王嗎？ Nǐmen dōu xìng Wáng ma? but not *你們都姓不姓王？ Nǐmen dōu xìng bú xìng Wáng?

4. When 都 *dōu* is modified by 不 *bù*, the sentence means 'not all....', e.g., 他們不都是臺灣人。Tāmen bù dōu shì Táiwān rén. 'Not all of them are Taiwanese'.

練習 Exercise

這三個人都是
日本人嗎？

這兩個人 ＿＿＿ ＿＿＿
喝茶。

這兩張照片 ＿＿＿ ＿＿＿
我姐姐的（照片）。

❶ 你是老師，他是老師。

→你們 ＿＿＿＿＿＿＿＿＿＿＿＿＿＿＿ 。

❷ 我喜歡喝咖啡，他喜歡喝咖啡。

→我們 ＿＿＿＿＿＿＿＿＿＿＿＿＿＿＿ 。

❸ 你沒有兄弟姐妹，你的老師沒有兄弟姐妹。

→你們 ＿＿＿＿＿＿＿＿＿＿＿＿＿＿＿ 。

❹ 你不要照相，他不要照相。

→你們 ＿＿＿＿＿＿＿＿＿＿＿＿＿＿＿ 。

V. Measures 個 ge and 張 zhāng 🎧 02-09

Function: Both 個 *ge* and 張 *zhāng* are measures. When indicating a quantity, a measure word is placed between the number and the noun.

1 一個哥哥

yí ge gēge

one brother

2 兩張好看的照片

liǎng zhāng hǎokàn de zhàopiàn

two pretty photos

3 幾個老師？

Jǐ ge lǎoshī?

How many teachers?

4 哪三個人？

Nǎ sān ge rén?

Which three people?

Structures:

1. Number + Measure + Noun

(1) 三個人

sān ge rén

three people

(2) 幾張照片？

Jǐ zhāng zhàopiàn?

How many photos?

2. Determiner + Number + Measure + Noun

(1) 哪一張照片？

Nǎ yì zhāng zhàopiàn?

Which photo?

When the number following 哪 *nǎ* is 一 *yī* 'one', the number is often omitted. For example, 哪一個人？ *Nǎ yí ge rén?* 'which person?' is the same as 哪個人？ *Něi ge rén?*.

Usage:

1. There are many measure words in Chinese. Different measure words are used with different nouns. In this lesson, only two measure words are introduced. 個 *ge* is the most frequently used measure word and is used as the measure for many different nouns. 張 *zhāng* is usually used with nouns that designate flat objects such as paper, photographs, and tables. When learning a new noun, you need to pay attention to the measure words that can be used with it.

2. When the numeral is "two", you do not say " 二 *èr* + measure + noun", rather you say " 兩 *liǎng* + measure + noun",

e.g.,　兩 + Measure + Noun

兩　個　　　妹妹　　　liǎng ge mèimei (two younger sisters)
兩　個　　　日本人　　liǎng ge Rìběn rén (two Japanese people)
兩　張　　　照片　　　liǎng zhāng zhàopiàn (two photos)

練習 Exercise

Place numbers and measure words in the blanks based on the nouns shown in the pictures.

❶

一 ＿＿＿＿ 人

❷

＿＿＿＿ ＿＿＿＿ 房子

❸

＿＿＿＿ ＿＿＿＿ 照片

❹

我有 ＿＿＿＿ ＿＿＿＿ 弟弟。

❺

＿＿＿＿ ＿＿＿＿ 很好看的 日本小姐

❻

＿＿＿＿ ＿＿＿＿ 漂亮的照片

Classroom Activities

I. Counting from 1 to 10

1	2	3	4	5	6	7	8	9	10
一	二	三	四	五	六	七	八	九	十
yī	èr	sān	sì	wǔ	liù	qī	bā	jiǔ	shí

II. Other People's Families

Goal: Learning to ask about people in your friend's family.

Task: Ask your classmates the following questions. Write down what you find out.

	問題 Question	例子 Example	同學一 Classmate 1	同學二 Classmate 2
1	你家有幾個人？	五個人		
2	你有沒有兄弟姐妹？	有 ＿ 個哥哥／姐姐／弟弟／妹妹		
3	你的兄弟姐妹是老師嗎？	是		
4	你有你家人的照片嗎？有幾張？	有，十張		
5	你家人都喜歡喝咖啡嗎？	爸爸喜歡，媽媽不喜歡。		
6	你家人都喜歡照相嗎？	我家人都不喜歡。		

III. Introducing Your Family

Goal: Learning to talk about family members' likes/dislikes.

Task: While one person introduces his/her family, other students complete the table below using information provided by the speaker. (Fill in the form using Chinese characters or pinyin.)

	名字 Name	國 Country	家人 Family members	哪個家人喜歡照相？ Who likes to take pictures?	哪個家人喜歡喝咖啡？ Who likes coffee?	哪個家人有很多書？ Who has a lot of books?
1						
2						
3						
4						
5						
6						

IV. People, Things, and Events

Goal: Use simple sentences to describe people, things, and events.

Task: Pair up with a partner and discuss the following questions based on the pictures provided below. Then tell the class your results of your discussion.

1 哪一張照片漂亮？

Nǎ yì zhāng zhàopiàn piàoliàng?

Which photo is pretty?

哥哥的照片　　姐姐的照片

2 他們是誰？

Tāmen shì shéi?

Who are they?

李明華　　白如玉

3 誰的書很多？

Shéi de shū hěn duō?

Who has a lot of books?

馬安同　　張怡君

4 誰的爸爸喜歡照相？

Shéi de bàba xǐhuān zhàoxiàng?

Whose dad likes to take pictures?

陳月美 的爸爸　　張怡君 的爸爸

5 誰不喜歡看書？

Shéi bù xǐhuān kànshū?

Who doesn't like to read?

馬安同　　張怡君

6 誰有好喝的茶？

Shéi yǒu hǎohē de chá?

Who has good-tasting tea?

李明華　　陳月美

文化 *Bits of Chinese Culture*

Family Central to Chinese Culture

The Chinese have a strong sense of family and parents frequently want to live with their children, especially with their sons. In old times, when sons married, they almost always lived with their parents. Parents also generally left their property to their sons, while daughters "belonged to somebody else" after they got married, so they did not live with their parents and, of course, they did not receive any inheritance. As times have changed and society has moved toward gender equality and lower birth rates, the situation is much different with sons and daughters now having the same

▲ Family get together

obligations and rights. You rarely see families with three generations living under one roof today. After they get married, some young people find a place near or even next door to their parents, mainly so that they can look after each other on a daily basis. In the past, when young couples in Taiwan had children, they would give them over to their parents to take care of, because they did not have to worry as much and it was less expensive than leaving them with a nanny. Obviously, many grandmothers and grandfathers were happy to be able to dote over their grandchildren. However, in order not to overtire their elderly parents, many choose to find for a nanny to take care of their kids or take them to preschool or a daycare center. It is also becoming increasingly common for Taiwanese to marry later or not at all. Many unmarried children in their 30s and 40s work away from home and live alone in rented rooms, making it impossible to live with or near their parents. This is much different from the past when parents and children lived together.

▲ Family trip

▲ Family celebration

Notes on Pinyin and Pronunciation

1. Pinyin Rules:

   When the vowel "i" stands alone (without a consonant in front of it), it is spelled yī（一）. When the vowel "u" stands alone, it is spelled wǔ（五）.

2. Tone Changes for 一 Yī

   (1) When 一 is used in names or in ordinal number, its tone does not undergo changes, e.g. Tiánzhōng Chéngyī（田中誠一）and dì yī kè（第一課）.

   (2) When 一 yī is used to signify an amount (followed by quantifiers) or when it appears in multisyllabic words, it follows the same tone change rules as 不 bù.

一 yī + 1st, 2nd or 3rd tone→ 4th tone (4th tone mark)		一 yī + 4th tone or neutral tone → 2nd tone (2nd tone mark)
` `	一 張 (M) 支 (M)（L4） 千 (N)（L4） ˇ 起 （L3） ˇ 種 (M)（L4）百 (N)（L4） 一	個 (M) ˊ ˋ 一 共（L4）

Note: When pronouncing "-o," it is natural to pronounce it with a slight "u", as in 伯 b(u)ó, 週末 zhōum(u)ò in Lesson Three, and 微波 wéib(u)ō in Lesson Four.

Introduction to Chinese Characters

Basic Structures of Chinese Characters:

	一 yī	人 rén	日 rì		李 lǐ	要 yào	兄 xiōng	是 shì
	你 nǐ	姓 xìng	都 dōu		茶 chá			
	咖 kā	謝 xiè	們 men		國 guó			

	這 zhè 迎 yíng 起 qǐ			麼 me 房 fáng 有 yǒu
	氣 qì 包 bāo 可 kě			同 tóng 問 wèn 間 jiān
	幽 yōu			區 qū

Basic Template for Chinese Calligraphy

To write beautiful Chinese characters, tidiness, balance, symmetry, and harmony are important. Nine-square grids are used to practice writing characters to achieve balanced beauty.

Nine-square grids used for writing practice consist of nine boxes in 3x3 grids. Since Chinese characters can be as simple as " 一 " or as complicated as " 謝 ", to achieve balance, symmetry, harmony, and fullness, they must occupy the same amount of space, regardless of how many strokes they have, when written in 3x3 grids.

Nine-square grids are a basic tool used for practicing the writing of Chinese characters. Beginners who use the grids to help them layout the structure of Chinese characters will eventually achieve balance in their writing.

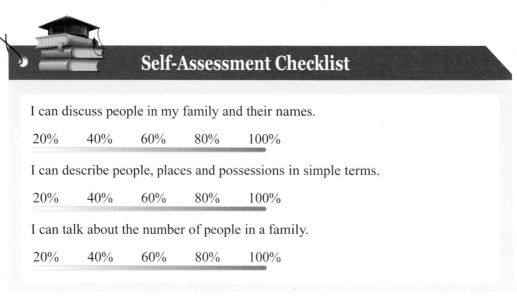

Self-Assessment Checklist

I can discuss people in my family and their names.

20%   40%   60%   80%   100%

I can describe people, places and possessions in simple terms.

20%   40%   60%   80%   100%

I can talk about the number of people in a family.

20%   40%   60%   80%   100%

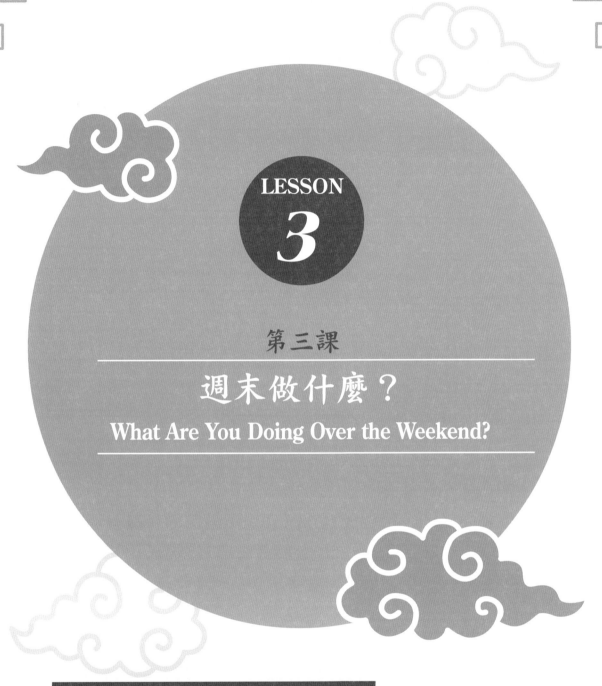

LESSON 3

第三課

週末做什麼？
What Are You Doing Over the Weekend?

學習目標 Learning Objectives

Topic: 喜好 Hobbies

- Learning to describe likes/dislikes (e.g., sports and movies).
- Learning to express what two groups have in common.
- Learning to politely ask others their opinions and make simple suggestions.
- Learning to form choice questions.

週末做什麼？

What Are You Doing Over the Weekend?

對話一 Dialogue 1 03-01 03-A

安　同：田中，你喜歡聽音樂嗎？
Āntóng ： Tiánzhōng, nǐ xǐhuān tīng yīnyuè ma?

田　中：我不喜歡聽音樂。我喜歡運動。
Tiánzhōng ： Wǒ bù xǐhuān tīng yīnyuè. Wǒ xǐhuān yùndòng.

安　同：你喜歡打網球嗎？
Āntóng ： Nǐ xǐhuān dǎ wǎngqiú ma?

田　中：我不喜歡打網球。
Tiánzhōng ： Wǒ bù xǐhuān dǎ wǎngqiú.

安　同：你喜歡做什麼？
Āntóng ： Nǐ xǐhuān zuò shénme?

田　中：打棒球和游泳，你呢？
Tiánzhōng ： Dǎ bàngqiú hàn yóuyǒng, nǐ ne?

安　同：我常打籃球，也常踢足球。
Āntóng　：Wǒ cháng dǎ lánqiú, yě cháng tī zúqiú.

田　中：我覺得踢足球很好玩。
Tiánzhōng　：Wǒ juéde tī zúqiú hěn hǎowán.

安　同：明天是週末，我們早上去踢足球，怎麼樣？
Āntóng　：Míngtiān shì zhōumò, wǒmen zǎoshàng qù tī zúqiú, zěnmeyàng?

田　中：好啊！
Tiánzhōng　：Hǎo a!

課文英譯 Text in English

Antong　： Tianzhong, do you like listening to music?

Tianzhong： I don't like listening to music. I like to exercise.

Antong　： Do you like to play tennis?

Tianzhong： I don't like to play tennis.

Antong　： What do you like to do?

Tianzhong： Play baseball and swim. And you?

Antong　： I often play basketball and also often play soccer.

Tianzhong： I think soccer is fun.

Antong　： The weekend is tomorrow. How about we go play soccer tomorrow morning?

Tianzhong： Great!

生詞一 Vocabulary 1 🎧 03-02

Vocabulary

1	週末	zhōumò	ㄓㄡ ㄇㄛˋ	(N)	weekend
2	聽	tīng	ㄊㄧㄥ	(V)	to listen
3	音樂	yīnyuè	ㄧㄣ ㄩㄝˋ	(N)	music
4	運動	yùndòng	ㄩㄣˋ ㄉㄨㄥˋ	(Vi)	to exercise
5	打	dǎ	ㄉㄚˇ	(V)	to play (ball games)
6	網球	wǎngqiú	ㄨㄤˇ ㄑㄧㄡˊ	(N)	tennis
7	棒球	bàngqiú	ㄅㄤˋ ㄑㄧㄡˊ	(N)	baseball
8	和	hàn	ㄏㄢˋ	(Conj)	and, as well as
9	游泳	yóuyǒng	ㄧㄡˊ ㄩㄥˇ	(V-sep)	to swim
10	常	cháng	ㄔㄤˊ	(Adv)	often
11	籃球	lánqiú	ㄌㄢˊ ㄑㄧㄡˊ	(N)	basketball
12	也	yě	ㄧㄝˇ	(Adv)	also
13	踢	tī	ㄊㄧ	(V)	to kick
14	足球	zúqiú	ㄗㄨˊ ㄑㄧㄡˊ	(N)	soccer
15	覺得	juéde	ㄐㄩㄝˊ ㄉㄜ	(Vst)	to feel, to think
16	好玩	hǎowán	ㄏㄠˇ ㄨㄢˊ	(Vs)	interesting, fun
17	明天	míngtiān	ㄇㄧㄥˊ ㄊㄧㄢ	(N)	tomorrow
18	早上	zǎoshàng	ㄗㄠˇ ㄕㄤˋ	(N)	morning
19	去	qù	ㄑㄩˋ	(V)	to go
20	怎麼樣	zěnmeyàng	ㄗㄣˇ ㄇㄜ ㄧㄤˋ	(Vs)	How about it? How does that sound? What do you think?
21	啊	a	ㄚ˙	(Ptc)	sentence-final particle

Phrases

22	做什麼	zuò shénme	ㄗㄨㄛˋ ㄕㄣˊ ㄇㄜ˙		do what
23	好啊	hǎo a	ㄏㄠˇ ㄚ˙		OK

對話二 Dialogue 2 03-03 03-B

如　玉：今天 晚上 我們 去 看 電影，好 不 好？
Rúyù　：Jīntiān wǎnshàng wǒmen qù kàn diànyǐng, hǎo bù hǎo?

月　美：好 啊！
Yuèměi　：Hǎo a!

如　玉：妳 想 看 美國 電影 還是 臺灣 電影？
Rúyù　：Nǐ xiǎng kàn Měiguó diànyǐng háishì Táiwān diànyǐng?

月　美：美國 電影、臺灣 電影，我 都 想 看。
Yuèměi　：Měiguó diànyǐng, Táiwān diànyǐng, wǒ dōu xiǎng kàn.

如　玉：我們 看 臺灣 電影 吧！
Rúyù　：Wǒmen kàn Táiwān diànyǐng ba!

月　美：好 啊！看 電影 可以 學 中文。
Yuèměi　：Hǎo a! Kàn diànyǐng kěyǐ xué Zhōngwén.

如　玉：晚上 要 不 要 一起 吃 晚飯？
Rúyù　：Wǎnshàng yào bú yào yìqǐ chī wǎnfàn?

月　美：好，我們 去 吃 越南 菜。
Yuèměi　：Hǎo, wǒmen qù chī Yuènán cài.

課文英譯 Text in English

Ruyu	:	Let's go see a movie tonight, OK?
Yuemei	:	Sure.
Ruyu	:	Do you want to see an American movie or a Taiwanese movie?
Yuemei	:	Either an American movie or a Taiwanese film is fine with me.
Ruyu	:	Let's go ahead and see a Taiwanese movie.
Yuemei	:	That's fine. Watching movies, I can learn Chinese.
Ruyu	:	Would you like to have dinner together tonight?
Yuemei	:	Okay. Let's go have Vietnamese food.

生詞二 Vocabulary 2   03-04

People in the dialogue

1	白如玉	Bái Rúyù	ㄅㄞˊ ㄖㄨˊ ㄩˋ		a woman from the US

Vocabulary

2	今天	jīntiān	ㄐㄧㄣ ㄊㄧㄢ	(N)	today
3	晚上	wǎnshàng	ㄨㄢˇ ㄕㄤˋ	(N)	evening, night
4	看	kàn	ㄎㄢˋ	(V)	to see, to watch
5	電影	diànyǐng	ㄉㄧㄢˋ ㄧㄥˇ	(N)	movie
6	妳	nǐ	ㄋㄧˇ	(N)	you (female)
7	想	xiǎng	ㄒㄧㄤˇ	(Vaux)	to want, to think
8	還是	háishì	ㄏㄞˊ ㄕˋ	(Conj)	or (used in a question)
9	吧	ba	ㄅㄚ˙	(Ptc)	sentence-final particle for suggestion
10	可以	kěyǐ	ㄎㄜˇ ㄧˇ	(Vaux)	could (possibility)
11	學	xué	ㄒㄩㄝˊ	(V)	to learn, to study
12	中文	Zhōngwén	ㄓㄨㄥ ㄨㄣˊ	(N)	Chinese language
13	一起	yìqǐ	ㄧˋ ㄑㄧˇ	(Adv)	together
14	吃	chī	ㄔ	(V)	to eat

| 15 | 晚飯 | wǎnfàn | ㄨㄢˇ ㄈㄢˋ | (N) | dinner |
| 16 | 菜 | cài | ㄘㄞˋ | (N) | cuisine |

Names

| 17 | 越南 | Yuènán | ㄩㄝˋ ㄋㄢˊ | | Vietnam |

Phrases

| 18 | 好不好 | hǎo bù hǎo | ㄏㄠˇ ㄨˋ ㄏㄠˇ | | How about...? How does that sound? |

文法 Grammar

I. Placement of Time Words 🎧 03-05

Structures: Time words appear after (mostly) or before (less commonly) the subject.

❶ 我們今天去看電影。

Wǒmen jīntiān qù kàn diànyǐng.

We went to see a movie today.

❷ 你明天想去游泳嗎？

Nǐ míngtiān xiǎng qù yóuyǒng ma?

Would you like to go swimming tomorrow?

❸ 週末他要去打籃球。

Zhōumò tā yào qù dǎ lánqiú.

This weekend, he is going to go play basketball.

❹ 明天你想做什麼？

Míngtiān nǐ xiǎng zuò shénme?

What would you like to do tomorrow?

Usage: Units of time in a series are expressed from larger to smaller. For example,

1. 明天晚上 míngtiān wǎnshàng (tomorrow evening)

   *晚上明天

2. 週末早上 zhōumò zǎoshàng (in the morning on the weekend)

   *早上週末

練習 Exercise

Complete with time words and sentences.

	S	TW	VP
1	我哥哥	週末	要去打籃球。
2	我們	_____	想去看電影。
3	你	_____	想吃越南菜還是臺灣菜？
4	我們	_____	去看電影還是去看 _____ ？
5	李先生	_____	_____ ？

	TW	S	VP
1	週末	你	要做什麼？
2	_____	我們	去他家。
3	_____	他	想吃越南菜。
4	_____	你	要去看電影嗎？
5	_____	王小姐	_____ 。

II. To Go Do Something with 去 qù 🎧 03-06

Function: 去 qù + VP indicates the intention to go do something.

1 我去打網球。
Wǒ qù dǎ wǎngqiú.
I am going to go play tennis.

2 他去踢足球。
Tā qù tī zúqiú.
He went to play soccer.

3 我們和老師都去看電影。
Wǒmen hàn lǎoshī dōu qù kàn diànyǐng.
We and the teacher are all going to go see a movie.

Structures: Negation markers, auxiliary verbs, and adverbs are placed before 去 *qù*.

✎ Negation:

1 我不去打籃球。
Wǒ bú qù dǎ lánqiú.
I am not going to go play basketball.

2 明天早上我不去游泳。
Míngtiān zǎoshàng wǒ bú qù yóuyǒng.
I am not going to go swimming tomorrow morning.

✎ Questions:

1 你要去看電影嗎？
Nǐ yào qù kàn diànyǐng ma?
Would you like to go see a movie?

2 你們常去吃越南菜嗎？
Nǐmen cháng qù chī Yuènán cài ma?
Do you often go eat Vietnamese food?

3 他不去打棒球嗎？
Tā bú qù dǎ bàngqiú ma?
Is he not going to go play baseball?

練習 Exercise

Complete the sentences below based on the pictures provided using 去＋ VP.

1 明天早上我們一起去 ＿＿＿＿＿＿＿＿＿＿＿＿。

2 今天晚上我不想 ＿＿＿＿＿＿＿＿ ＿＿＿＿＿＿＿＿。

3 你週末常 ＿＿＿＿＿＿＿ ＿＿＿＿＿＿＿ 嗎？

4 我妹妹今天晚上要 ＿＿＿＿＿＿＿ ＿＿＿＿＿＿＿。

5 我爸爸去打棒球，我哥哥 ＿＿＿＿＿＿＿ ＿＿＿＿＿＿＿。

III. Topic Sentences 🎧 03-07

Function: When you want to describe, explain, or evaluate a person, event, or thing, you place the person, event, or thing at the beginning of the sentence as the "topic". The rest of the sentence serves as the "comment". The topic of a sentence is usually the person or thing that is placed at the beginning of the sentence.

❶ A：臺灣人喜歡喝烏龍茶嗎？
Táiwān rén xǐhuān hē Wūlóng chá ma?
Do Taiwanese people like to drink Oolong tea?

B：烏龍茶，臺灣人都喜歡喝。
Wūlóng chá, Táiwān rén dōu xǐhuān hē.
Oolong tea, Taiwanese people all like to drink (it).

❷ A：你有哥哥、姐姐嗎？
Nǐ yǒu gēge, jiějie ma?
Do you have any brothers and sisters?

B：哥哥、姐姐，我都沒有。
Gēge, jiějie, wǒ dōu méiyǒu.
Brothers, sisters, I have none.

❸ A：你想看美國電影還是臺灣電影？
Nǐ xiǎng kàn Měiguó diànyǐng háishì Táiwān diànyǐng?
Do you want to watch an American movie or a Taiwanese movie?

B：美國電影、臺灣電影，我都想看。
Měiguó diànyǐng, Táiwān diànyǐng, wǒ dōu xiǎng kàn.
American movie, Taiwanese movie, I would like to watch either.

Structures: Topics are always placed at the very beginning of a sentence.

❶ 打棒球，我不喜歡。
Dǎ bàngqiú, wǒ bù xǐhuān.
Playing baseball, I don't like (it).

❷ 越南菜，我常吃。
Yuènán cài, wǒ cháng chī.
Vietnamese food, I often eat (it).

❸ 這張照片，我覺得很好看。
Zhè zhāng zhàopiàn, wǒ juéde hěn hǎokàn.
This photo, I think (it) is quite nice.

Usage: In a topic-comment sentence, if the fronted object consists of a collective noun, or more than one noun, the totality marker, 都 *dōu* is required.

❶ 中國菜，我都喜歡吃。（collective noun）
Zhōngguó cài, wǒ dōu xǐhuān chī.
Chinese food, I like to eat (them) all.

2 弟弟、妹妹，我都有。（two object nouns）

Dìdi, mèimei, wǒ dōu yǒu.

Younger brothers and younger sisters, I've got both.

練習 Exercise

Complete the topic-comment sentences.

1 我常看美國電影。　　　→ ＿＿＿＿＿＿＿，我常看。

2 我覺得踢足球很好玩。→ ＿＿＿＿＿＿＿，我覺得很好玩。

3 A：你喜歡喝臺灣茶還是日本茶？

B：＿＿＿＿ 茶、＿＿＿＿ 茶，我都不喝。

4 A：你喜歡越南菜還是臺灣菜？

B：＿＿＿＿ 和 ＿＿＿＿ ，我 ＿＿＿＿＿＿＿。

5 A：你有弟弟和妹妹嗎？

B：＿＿＿＿ 和 ＿＿＿＿ ，我 ＿＿＿＿＿＿＿。

6 A：網球、籃球，你都喜歡嗎？

B：＿＿＿＿＿ ，我喜歡；＿＿＿＿＿ ，我 ＿＿＿＿＿＿＿。

IV. The Word Order of Adverbs 也 yě, 都 dōu and 常 cháng　🎧 03-08

Structures:

1. 也 *yě*, 都 *dōu* and 常 *cháng* are adverbs. Adverbs modify verbs. Adverbs always occur before the verb in Chinese.

也 *yě* ／ 都 *dōu* ／ 常 *cháng* + VP

	Subject	Predicate	
		Adv(s)	VP
我是美國人，	他	也	是美國人。
我姐姐很漂亮，	我妹妹	也很	漂亮。
	我和王老師	都	喜歡他。
	你家人	都很	好看。
	我	常	打網球。

2. When 也 *yě* and either 都 *dōu* or 常 *cháng* occur in a sentence together to modify the VP, 也 *yě* is placed before 都 *dōu* or 常 *cháng*.

	Subject	Predicate	
		Adv(s)	VP
我是日本人，	他們	也都	是日本人。
我家人喜歡照相，	他家人	也都	喜歡照相。
你很喜歡吃越南菜，	我們	也都很	喜歡吃越南菜。
你常喝咖啡，	我	也常	喝咖啡。
你常去踢足球，	我們	也都常	去踢足球。

✎ **Negation:** In negation, 也 *yě* is placed before the negation markers 不 *bù* / 沒 *méi*, while 常 *cháng* is placed after 不 *bù*. 都 *dōu* can occur before or after 不 *bù*, but it changes the meaning of the sentence.

1 我不是日本人，他也不是日本人。

Wǒ bú shì Rìběn rén, tā yě bú shì Rìběn rén.

I am not Japanese and he is not, either.

2 我沒有弟弟，也沒有妹妹。

Wǒ méi yǒu dìdi, yě méi yǒu mèimei.

I don't have a younger brother or a younger sister.

❸ 他不喜歡看電影，我也不
喜歡看電影。

Tā bù xǐhuān kàn diànyǐng, wǒ yě bù
xǐhuān kàn diànyǐng.

He doesn't like to watch movies and I
don't like to watch movies, either.

❺ 我們都不是美國人。

Wǒmen dōu bú shì Měiguó rén.

None of us is American.

❹ 我不常看電影。

Wǒ bù cháng kàn diànyǐng.

I don't watch movies often.

❻ 他們不都是美國人。
（有美國人，也有日本人。）

Tāmen bù dōu shì Měiguó rén. (Yǒu
Měiguó rén, yě yǒu Rìběn rén.)

Not all of them are American. (There are
Americans, and there are Japanese.)

練習 Exercise

Complete with 也 , 都 or 常 .

❶ 陳先生喜歡喝茶，_____ 喜歡喝咖啡。

❷ 我 _____ 喝咖啡，也 _____ 喝茶。

❸ 我不是日本人，他 _____ 不是日本人。

❹ 我沒有哥哥，_____ 沒有姐姐。

❺ 他的家人都喜歡打網球，我家人也 _____ 喜歡打網球。

❻ 我們 _____ 不常踢足球。

❼ 我不 _____ 游泳。

V. Making Suggestions 吧 ba 🎧 03-09

Function: 吧 *ba* indicates a suggestion from the speaker.

❶ A：我們去喝咖啡還是喝茶？

Wǒmen qù hē kāfēi háishì hē chá?

Shall we go drink coffee or tea?

B：我們去喝咖啡吧。

Wǒmen qù hē kāfēi ba.

Let's go drink coffee.

❷ A：今天晚上我們看什麼電影？

Jīntiān wǎnshàng wǒmen kàn shénme diànyǐng?

What movie are we watching tonight?

B：我們去看臺灣電影吧！

Wǒmen qù kàn Táiwān diànyǐng ba.

Let's watch a Taiwanese movie.

❸ A：週末我們去打籃球，好不好？

Zhōumò wǒmen qù dǎ lánqiú, hǎo bù hǎo?

Let's go play basketball on the weekend, OK?

B：我不喜歡打籃球，我們打網球吧！

Wǒ bù xǐhuān dǎ lánqiú, wǒmen dǎ wǎngqiú ba!

I don't like to play basketball. Let's play tennis.

Structures: 吧 *ba* is placed at the sentence-final position.

Usage: 吧 *ba* is used in imperatives to soften the command. For example, 喝吧。 *Hē ba.* An imperative without 吧 *ba* sounds harsh and direct and can be impolite, for example, 喝！ *Hē!*

練習 Exercise

Complete with suitable suggestions.

	A	B…吧
1	我們喝什麼茶？	我們喝烏龍茶吧！
2	我們吃什麼？	我們吃臺灣菜吧！
3	我們看什麼電影？	我們看美國電影吧！

❶ A：我們明天晚上看什麼電影？

　 B：我想學中文，我們 ＿＿＿＿＿＿＿＿＿＿＿＿＿ 吧。

❷ A：我們週末要做什麼？

　 B：＿＿＿＿＿＿＿＿＿＿＿＿＿＿＿＿＿ 。

Classroom Activities

I. What Does This Person Like to Do?

Goal: Learning to describe what kind of sports or activities a person likes.

Task 1: Look at the pictures below and say what the person in the picture often does in the morning and in the evening. What did he do today?

	Mon.	Tue.	Wed.	Thu. 今天	Fri.	Sun.
早上 Morning						
晚上 Evening						

Task 2: Look at the pictures again and answer the following questions.

1 他常看電影還是常打籃球？ **2** 他常踢足球還是常游泳？

3 他今天打網球還是打籃球？

II. Making Suggestions

Goal: Learning to ask someone's opinion in a polite way and offer a suggestion.

Task: Tomorrow is the weekend. Discuss what to do on the weekend with your classmates. Have three students role play the conversation below, using the pictures above.

A：明天是週末，我們做什麼？
B：我們去 ＿＿＿＿＿＿＿ 吧！
C：我不喜歡 ＿＿＿＿＿＿＿，我們 ＿＿＿＿＿＿＿ 吧！
A：我不喜歡 ＿＿＿＿＿＿＿，我們 ＿＿＿＿＿＿＿，好不好？
B：好，我們一起去 ＿＿＿＿＿＿＿ ！

III. Find What You Have in Common

Goal: Learning to talk about what two people or groups of people have in common.

Task: Look at the chart below and try to discover what the people listed on it have in common. Do not repeat common points that somebody has already mentioned.

Example

❶ 我常喝咖啡，小王也常喝咖啡。

Wǒ cháng hē kāfēi, XiǎoWáng yě cháng hē kāfēi.

I often drink coffee. Xiao Wang also drinks coffee often.

❷ 我們和他弟弟都很常游泳。

Wǒmen hàn tā dìdi dōu hěn cháng yóuyǒng.

We and his brother often go swimming.

	常喝咖啡	喜歡看電影	喜歡喝茶	不常打棒球	常打網球	喜歡打籃球	常踢足球	常游泳	很好看	不是日本人	美國人
我	✓		✓								
你		✓		✓			✓		✓		✓
他				✓						✓	
我們								✓		✓	
他們		✓				✓					
你家人						✓			✓		
他弟弟				✓				✓			
我妹妹					✓						
開文							✓				✓
小王	✓		✓								

IV. Survey

Goal: Learning to ask and reply to choice questions (choosing between two or more items).

Task: This is a survey. Ask your classmates questions using the activities shown in the squares below as prompts and report your findings.

Example

A：你喜歡打籃球還是踢足球？

Nǐ xǐhuān dǎ lánqiú háishì tī zúqiú?

Do you like to play basketball or soccer?

B：我喜歡打籃球，也喜歡踢足球。

Wǒ xǐhuān dǎ lánqiú, yě xǐhuān tī zúqiú.

I like basketball and also like soccer.

我喜歡打籃球，不喜歡踢足球。

Wǒ xǐhuān dǎ lánqiú, bù xǐhuān tī zúqiú.

I like basketball. I don't like soccer.

打籃球、踢足球，我都不喜歡。

Dǎ lánqiú, tī zúqiú, wǒ dōu bù xǐhuān.

Both basketball and soccer, I don't like.

Write the number of people that like the various activities below in the boxes provided and report your findings.

Example

五個人喜歡打籃球。

Wǔ ge rén xǐhuān dǎ lánqiú.

Five people like to play basketball.

兩個人不常喝茶。

Liǎng ge rén bù cháng hē chá.

Two people seldom drink tea.

	喜歡	不喜歡	結果（Results）
打籃球			
踢足球			
吃臺灣菜			
吃日本菜			
美國電影			
日本電影			
臺灣電影			
	常	不常	結果（Results）
游泳			
打網球			
喝咖啡			
喝茶			

A One-of-a-kind Leisure Activity—Shrimp Fishing

Shrimp fishing is a one-of-a-kind leisure activity found only in Taiwan. It is popular among locals and foreigners living in Taiwan and can be found on many travel itineraries for tourists.

▲ Shrimp-fishing site

The shrimp caught at shrimp-fishing sites are raised specifically for that purpose. The facilities are open to the public who is charged by the hour. Shrimp fishing originated in southern Taiwan in the 1980s and gradually spread to the rest of Taiwan. The first venues were outdoors, but shrimp fishing eventually became an indoor activity as enthusiasts wanted to stay out of the sun and weather. An indoor shrimp-fishing facility is a great place to spend half a day. You can roast the shrimp you catch or have them roasted by the staff and eat them right there.

There are many ways to cook shrimp, but nothing beats eating roasted shrimp and drinking beer. This laid-back leisure activity is a good way to relieve stress and a great escape from the hustle and bustle of daily life.

▲ Shrimp-fishing

▲ Shrimp caught

▲ Shrimp ready to roast

▲ Roasted shrimp

攝影：王盈雯、林蔚儒、《聯合報》廖雅欣

61

Notes on Pinyin and Pronunciation

Pinyin Rules:

When the vowel "ü" is preceded by the consonant "j", "q", or "x," the umlaut (the two dots above the letter) is omitted, e.g., jué（覺）. When it is not preceded by any consonant, it is spelled yù （玉）.

When the vowel "i" is followed by the vowel "a", "o", or "e" and is not preceded by consonant, change the "i" to a "y", e.g., -iao → yào（要）, -ie → yě（也）.

Introduction to Chinese Characters

Using Components to Learn Chinese Characters

Learning Chinese characters requires familiarizing yourself with their pronunciations, meanings, and form. The form (structure of Chinese characters) consists of structures with three tiers: the entire character itself, components, and strokes.

Components are the basic units of Chinese characters

Components are the smallest writing unit to Chinese characters. They fall between strokes and radicals (strokes ≦ components ≦ radicals) and are the core structures of Chinese writing. Independent characters have only one component and compound characters have at least two components. For example, the character in " 好 " has two components: " 女 " and " 子 ."

好＝女＋子

The character " 樂 "（happy）has three components: " 白 ," " 幺 ," and " 木 ."

樂＝白＋幺＋幺＋木

The most effective way to learn characters

Using components to learn Chinese characters helps the learner break down the complicated forms of characters and makes learning easier. Components also help the learner understand characteristics of Chinese characters and speeds up word recognition and learning, while helping build up word repertoire.

Self-Assessment Checklist

I can describe likes/dislikes (e.g., sports and movies).

20%   40%   60%   80%   100%

I can express what two groups have in common.

20%   40%   60%   80%   100%

I can politely ask other's opinions and make simple suggestions.

20%   40%   60%   80%   100%

I can form choice questions.

20%   40%   60%   80%   100%

LESSON 4

第四課

請問一共多少錢？
Excuse Me. How Much Does That Cost in Total?

Topic: 購物 Shopping

- Learning to ask and talk about prices.
- Learning to ask for reasons.
- Learning to use simple phrases to describe the size and function of common objects.

請問一共多少錢？

Excuse Me. How Much Does That Cost in Total?

對話一 Dialogue 1 🎧 04-01 AR 04-A

老　　闆	請問你要買什麼？
Lǎobǎn	Qǐngwèn nǐ yào mǎi shénme?
明　　華	一杯熱咖啡。兩個包子。
Mínghuá	Yì bēi rè kāfēi. Liǎng ge bāozi.
老　　闆	你要大杯、中杯還是小杯？
Lǎobǎn	Nǐ yào dà bēi, zhōng bēi háishì xiǎo bēi?
明　　華	大杯。包子請幫我微波。
Mínghuá	Dà bēi. Bāozi qǐng bāng wǒ wéibō.
老　　闆	好的。請問外帶還是內用？
Lǎobǎn	Hǎode. Qǐngwèn wàidài háishì nèiyòng?
明　　華	外帶，一共多少錢？
Mínghuá	Wàidài, yígòng duōshǎo qián?
老　　闆	咖啡八十，包子四十，一共一百二十塊。
Lǎobǎn	Kāfēi bāshí, bāozi sìshí, yígòng yìbǎi èrshí kuài.

課文英譯 Text in English

Store owner : Excuse me, what would you like (to order)?

Minghua : A cup of hot coffee and two baozi.

Store owner : Would you like a large, medium, or small cup?

Minghua : Large. Please microwave the baozi for me.

Store owner : OK. Excuse me. Is this to go or for here?

Minghua : To go. How much does that cost altogether?

Store owner : 80 for the coffee, 40 for the baozi. That will be 120 in total.

生詞一 Vocabulary 04-02

Vocabulary

1	一共	yígòng	ㄧˊ ㄍㄨㄥˋ	(Adv)	altogether
2	多少	duōshǎo	ㄉㄨㄛ ㄕㄠˇ	(N)	how much, how many
3	錢	qián	ㄑㄧㄢˊ	(N)	money
4	老闆	lǎobǎn	ㄌㄠˇ ㄅㄢˇ	(N)	store-owner, boss
5	買	mǎi	ㄇㄞˇ	(V)	to buy
6	杯	bēi	ㄅㄟ	(M)	cup
7	熱	rè	ㄖㄜˋ	(Vs)	hot
8	包子	bāozi	ㄅㄠ ㄗ˙	(N)	steamed buns with meat stuffing filling
9	要	yào	ㄧㄠˋ	(V)	to want, to need
10	大	dà	ㄉㄚˋ	(Vs)	large
11	中	zhōng	ㄓㄨㄥ	(Vs-attr)	medium
12	小	xiǎo	ㄒㄧㄠˇ	(Vs)	small
13	幫	bāng	ㄅㄤ	(Prep)	for
14	微波	wéibō	ㄨㄟˊ ㄅㄛ	(V)	to microwave
15	百	bǎi	ㄅㄞˇ	(N)	hundred
16	塊	kuài	ㄎㄨㄞˋ	(M)	measure word for Chinese money

Phrases

17	好的	hǎode	ㄏㄠˇ ㄉㄜ˙	OK
18	外帶	wàidài	ㄨㄞˋ ㄉㄞˋ	take out, to go
19	內用	nèiyòng	ㄋㄟˋ ㄩㄥˋ	for here

對話二 Dialogue 2 04-03 AR 04-B

月　　美：我想買一支新手機。
Yuèměi　：Wǒ xiǎng mǎi yì zhī xīn shǒujī.

明　　華：妳的手機很好。為什麼要買新的？
Mínghuá　：Nǐ de shǒujī hěn hǎo. Wèishénme yào mǎi xīn de?

月　　美：我這支手機太舊了，不好看。
Yuèměi　：Wǒ zhè zhī shǒujī tài jiù le, bù hǎokàn.

明　　華：妳想買哪種手機？
Mínghuá　：Nǐ xiǎng mǎi nǎ zhǒng shǒujī?

月　　美：能照相也能上網。
Yuèměi　：Néng zhàoxiàng yě néng shàngwǎng.

明　華 ： 那種手機很好，我哥哥有一支。
Mínghuá ： Nà zhǒng shǒujī hěn hǎo, wǒ gēge yǒu yì zhī.

月　美 ： 貴不貴？一支賣多少錢？
Yuèměi ： Guì bú guì? Yì zhī mài duōshǎo qián?

明　華 ： 那種手機不便宜。一支要一萬五千多。
Mínghuá ： Nà zhǒng shǒujī bù piányí. Yì zhī yào yíwàn wǔqiān duō.

課文英譯 Text in English

Yuemei ： I want to buy a new cell phone.

Minghua ： Your cell phone is fine. Why do you want to buy a new one?

Yuemei ： This one of mine is too old. It's unattractive.

Minghua ： What kind of cell phone do you want to buy?

Yuemei ： (One that) can take pictures and go online.

Minghua ： Those kinds of cell phones are good. My brother has one.

Yuemei ： Are they expensive? How much does one cost?

Minghua ： That kind of cell phone is not cheap. One costs over NT$15,000.

生詞二 Vocabulary 2 04-04

Vocabulary

1	支	zhī	ㄓ	(M)	measure word for cell phones
2	新	xīn	ㄒㄧㄣ	(Vs)	new
3	手機	shǒujī	ㄕㄡˇ ㄐㄧ	(N)	cell phone
4	太	tài	ㄊㄞˋ	(Adv)	too
5	舊	jiù	ㄐㄧㄡˋ	(Vs)	old
6	了	le	ㄌㄜ	(Ptc)	sentence-final particle indicating the speaker's sense of certainty

7	種	zhǒng	ㄓㄨㄥˇ	(M)	kind, type
8	能	néng	ㄋㄥˊ	(Vaux)	can, to be able to
9	上網	shàngwǎng	ㄕㄤˋ ㄨㄤˇ	(V-sep)	to access the internet, to use the internet
10	那	nà / nèi	ㄋㄚˋ / ㄋㄟˋ	(Det)	that
11	貴	guì	ㄍㄨㄟˋ	(Vs)	expensive
12	賣	mài	ㄇㄞˋ	(V)	to sell
13	便宜	piányí	ㄆㄧㄢˊ ㄧˊ	(Vs)	cheap, inexpensive
14	要	yào	ㄧㄠˋ	(Vst)	to take, to require
15	萬	wàn	ㄨㄢˋ	(N)	ten thousand
16	千	qiān	ㄑㄧㄢ	(N)	thousand

Phrases

| 17 | 為什麼 | wèishénme | ㄨㄟˋ ㄕㄣˊ ㄇㄜ˙ | | why |

文法 Grammar

I. Measures 塊 kuài, 杯 bēi, 支 zhī and 種 zhǒng 04-05

Structures:

1. A measure word is needed when a noun is modified by a number.

(1) 一杯咖啡 yì bēi kāfēi   one cup of coffee

(2) 十支手機 shí zhī shǒujī   ten (units of) cell phones

(3) 三個弟弟 sān ge dìdi   three younger brothers

2. Determiners 這 zhè, 那 nà, 哪 nǎ precede the words measures shown in Structure 1-(1), 一 yī is usually omitted.

Det + Numeral + Measure + N

(1) 這兩杯熱咖啡一共多少錢？

Zhè liǎng bēi rè kāfēi yígòng duōshǎo qián?

How much in total is it for these two cups of hot coffee?

(2) 那三支手機太舊了。

Nà sān zhī shǒujī tài jiù le.

Those three cell phones are too old.

(3) 哪（一）種手機不貴？

Nǎ (yì) zhǒng shǒujī bú guì?

Which type of cell phone is not expensive?

練習 Exercise

Please fill in the blanks with measure words.

1 一 _____ 熱咖啡三十五塊錢。

2 這兩 _____ 手機都能上網。

3 那十 _____ 臺灣人喜歡喝烏龍茶。

4 這 _____ 茶很好喝。

5 哪 _____ 包子好吃？

II. Preposition 幫 bāng *on behalf of* 🎧 04-06

Function: 幫 *bāng* introduces the beneficiary of an action.

1 請幫我微波包子。

Qǐng bāng wǒ wéibō bāozi.

Please microwave the baozi for me.

2 請幫我買一杯咖啡。

Qǐng bāng wǒ mǎi yì bēi kāfēi.

Please buy a cup of coffee for me.

3 請幫我照相。

Qǐng bāng wǒ zhàoxiàng.

Please take a picture for me.

Structures:

Negation: The negation marker 不 *bù* is placed before the preposition 幫 *bāng*, not before the verb.

❶ 他不幫我微波包子。　　（*他幫我不微波包子。）

Tā bù bāng wǒ wéibō bāozi .

He won't microwave the baozi for me.

❷ 姐姐不幫弟弟買咖啡。　（*姐姐幫弟弟不買咖啡。）

Jiějie bù bāng dìdi mǎi kāfēi.

Sister won't buy coffee for brother.

❸ 王先生不幫我照相。　　（*王先生幫我不照相。）

Wáng Xiānshēng bù bāng wǒ zhàoxiàng.

Mr. Wang would not take a picture for me.

✏️ Questions:

❶ 你幫不幫他買手機？

Nǐ bāng bù bāng tā mǎi shǒujī?

Are you going to buy a cell phone on his behalf?

❷ 他幫你照相嗎？

Tā bāng nǐ zhàoxiàng ma?

Did he take a photo for you?

❸ 誰能幫安同微波包子？

Shéi néng bāng Āntóng wéibō bāozi?

Who can microwave a baozi for Antong?

練習 Exercise

Complete the sentences below with the beneficiary 幫 bāng.

❶	❷	❸

包子不熱。	我想喝咖啡。	我們想照相。
請你 _____。	請你 _____。	請你 _____。

III. 的 De-phrase with the Head Noun Omitted 🎧 04-07

Function: Nouns are always 'modified' or described using this structure: modifier 的 + head noun. When the head noun is clear from the context, the head noun is often omitted.

1 A：你要買新手機還是舊手機？

        Nǐ yào mǎi xīn shǒujī háishì jiù shǒujī?

        Do you want to buy a new cell phone or an old one?

    B：我要新的，不要舊的。

        Wǒ yào xīn de, bú yào jiù de.

        I want a new one. I don't want an old one.

2 A：新手機貴不貴？

        Xīn shǒujī guì bú guì?

        Are new cell phones expensive?

    B：新的很貴。

        Xīn de hěn guì.

        New ones are expensive.

Structures:

✏️ Negation:

1 你的手機不是新的。

    Nǐ de shǒujī bú shì xīn de.

    Your cell phone is not new.

3 房子很貴，我不買大的。

    Fángzi hěn guì, wǒ bù mǎi dà de.

    Houses are expensive. I won't buy a large one.

2 這杯咖啡不熱，我要熱的。

    Zhè bēi kāfēi bú rè, wǒ yào rè de.

    This cup of coffee is not hot. I want a hot one.

Questions:

1 房子,你喜歡新的嗎?
Fángzi, nǐ xǐhuān xīn de ma?
House, do you like a new one?

2 手機,他買不買舊的?
Shǒujī, tā mǎi bù mǎi jiù de?
Cell phone, will he buy an old one?

3 咖啡,你要熱的嗎?
Kāfēi, nǐ yào rè de ma?
Coffee, do you want a cup of hot
one?

練習 Exercise

Complete the answers.

1 A:這杯茶熱,那杯不熱。你要哪一杯?

B:我要 _____。

2 A:王先生要買新手機還是舊手機?

B:他要買 _____。

3 A:新手機能上網,舊的不能上網。你要哪種?

B:我要 _____。

4 A:大杯熱茶 35 塊錢,小的 25 塊錢,你要買哪一杯?

B:我要 _____。

5 A:大的很貴,小的很便宜。你喜歡哪一個?

B:我喜歡 _____。

IV. 太 tài⋯了 le _overly_ 🎧 04-08

Function: 太 _tài_⋯了 _le_ indicates "too" or "overly", a negative observation given by
the speaker.

1 太貴了。 Tài guì le. (Too expensive.)

2 太大了。 Tài dà le. (Too big.)

3 太熱了。 Tài rè le. (Too hot.)

Usage:

1. "太 *tài* + Vs" means that a noun is "too" or "overly" (adj.). This pattern can also be used as a predicate, e.g., 那支手機太貴。Nà zhī shǒujī tài guì. 'That cell phone is too expensive'.

2. "太 *tài* + Vs + 了" is more subjective, indicating that the speaker feels that what is being talked about is excessively (adj.). For example, 那支手機太貴了。Nà zhī shǒujī tài guì le. 'That cell phone is way too expensive'.

練習 Exercise

Complete the answers below using "太…了" with the following words.

舊、貴、大、熱、小

1 A：你為什麼不買那種手機？　B：_____。

2 A：你喜歡吃大包子嗎？　B：不喜歡，_____。

3 A：你為什麼要買新手機？　B：我的手機_____，不好看。

4 A：你們為什麼不賣小杯咖啡？ B：_____，沒有人買。

5 A：你要喝熱咖啡嗎？　B：_____，我不要喝。

V. 能 néng *capability* 🎧 04-09

Function: The auxiliary verb 能 *néng* expresses some capability of the subject.

1 新手機能上網。
Xīn shǒujī néng shàngwǎng.
New cell phones can go online.

2 那支手機能照相。
Nà zhī shǒujī néng zhàoxiàng.
That cell phone can take photos.

75

Structures:

 Negation: The negation marker 不 *bù* should be placed before, and not after the auxiliary verb.

1 我的手機不能上網。
Wǒ de shǒujī bù néng shàngwǎng.
My cell phone cannot access the internet.

2 誰的手機不能照相？
Shéi de shǒujī bù néng zhàoxiàng?
Whose cell phone cannot take pictures?

 Questions: The auxiliary verb 能 *néng* is placed in the A position in the A-not-A pattern.

1 你的手機能不能照相？
Nǐ de shǒujī néng bù néng zhàoxiàng?
Can your cell phone take pictures?

2 舊的能不能上網？
Jiù de néng bù néng shàngwǎng?
Can the old one go online?

3 那支手機能不能上網？
Nà zhī shǒujī néng bù néng shàngwǎng?
Can that cell phone go online?

練習 Exercise

Look at the pictures and use 能 or 不能 to answer the questions.

哪種手機
能照相？
_____

他今天能不能
踢足球？
_____

 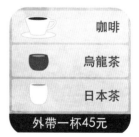
烏龍茶能不能
外帶？
_____

咖啡
烏龍茶
日本茶
外帶一杯45元

他能不能上網？

_____

老闆能不能幫他
微波包子？

_____

VI. 多 duō ...and more 04-10

Function: 多 *duō* is used after numbers to indicate "more than" or "over".

1 二十多個人
èrshí duō ge rén
20 some people

2 五萬多支手機
wǔ wàn duō zhī shǒujī
50,000 plus cell phone

Structures:

1. When 多 *duō* is associated with a number greater than 10, 多 indicates the residual amount.

數詞 numeral	多 more	量詞 measure	名詞 noun
二十	多	個	人
五百	多	個	包子
一千	多	支	手機
三萬四千	多	塊	錢

(1) 二十多個人
èrshí duō ge rén
over 20 people (but under 30)

(2) 一千多支手機
yìqiān duō zhī shǒujī
over 1,000 cell phones (but under 2,000)

(3) 五百多個包子
wǔbǎi duō ge bāozi
over 500 baozi (but under 600)

(4) 三萬四千多塊錢
sānwàn sìqiān duō kuài qián
over 34,000 dollars (but under 35,000)

2. When 多 *duō* is used with a number, it refers to what is not specified.

(1) 五塊多（錢）
wǔ kuài duō (qián)
more than five dollars (under 6)

(2) 一塊多（錢）
yí kuài duō (qián)
more than one dollar (under 2)

練習 Exercise

Complete responses as specified.

① 你賣多少手機？　一千兩百多支手機 （1,200 ～ 1,300）

② 你吃幾個包子？

＿＿＿＿＿＿＿＿＿＿＿＿＿＿＿＿＿ 。

③ 你有多少錢？ ＿＿＿＿＿＿＿＿＿ （50,000 ～ 55,000）

④ 他有幾塊錢？

＿＿＿＿＿＿＿＿＿＿＿ （7 ～ 8）

⑤ 那支手機賣多少錢？

＿＿＿＿＿＿＿＿＿＿＿ （21,000 ～ 22,000）

課 室 活 動 **Classroom Activities**

I. Ask and Talk about Prices

Goal: Learning to ask and talk about prices.

Task: Your classmate purchased something, so s/he knows the price. Ask him/her about the costs of the items below.

圖一　　　　　圖二　　　　　圖三　　　　　圖四

II. My Cell Phone

Goal: Learning to use simple phrases to describe the size and functions of common objects.

Task: Describe your cellphone, e.g., its size and what it can do.

III. Ask for Reasons

Goal: Learning to ask for reasons.

Task: You would like to buy a gift for your friend. Pair up with a classmate to discuss which cell phone is better. Say which cell phone you picked and explain why. Include at least the following grammatical patterns in your discussion:

這三支手機，你喜歡…，…，還是…？

為什麼？

…太…了

一支要…

IV. Counting from 11 to 110

Task: Fill in the missing numbers to 110.

11	12	13	14	15	16	17	18	19	20
十一 shíyī	十二 shí'èr	十三 shísān	十四 shísì	十五 shíwǔ	十六 shíliù	十七 shíqī	十八 shíbā	十九 shíjiǔ	二十 èrshí
21				**25**		**27**			**30**
二十一 èrshíyī				二十五 èrshíwǔ		二十七 èrshíqī			三十 sānshí
31			**34**				**38**		**40**
三十一 sānshíyī			三十四 sānshísì				三十八 sānshíbā		四十 sìshí
41	**42**	**43**			**46**				**50**
四十一 sìshíyī	四十二 sìshí'èr	四十三 sìshísān			四十六 sìshíliù				五十 wǔshí
51									**60**
五十一 wǔshíyī									六十 liùshí
61			**64**		**66**		**68**		**70**
六十一 liùshíyī			六十四 liùshísì		六十六 liùshíliù		六十八 liùshíbā		七十 qīshí
71		**73**		**75**		**77**			**80**
七十一 qīshíyī		七十三 qīshísān		七十五 qīshíwǔ		七十七 qīshíqī			八十 bāshí
81	**82**		**84**			**87**			**90**
八十一 bāshíyī	八十二 bāshí'èr		八十四 bāshísì			八十七 bāshíqī			九十 jiǔshí
91			**94**		**96**			**99**	**100**
九十一 jiǔshíyī			九十四 jiǔshísì		九十六 jiǔshíliù			九十九 jiǔshíjiǔ	一百 yìbǎi
101	**102**								**110**
一百零一 yìbǎi líng yī	一百零二 yìbǎi líng èr								一百一十 yìbǎi yīshí

0（零 líng）：zero

文化 *Bits of Chinese Culture*

Around-the-clock Convenience Stores

Students who are new to Taiwan can buy their meals without knowing a single word in Chinese. They can do this in any of Taiwan's 24/7 convenience stores. Many students will probably even miss the convenience of these stores after they have returned to their countries and wish that they could take the stores home with them.

▲ Fresh coffee sold at convenience stores

Convenience stores are very important to local life in Taiwan and offer an impressive range of services. You get full meals, snacks, drinks, stationary supplies, articles for daily use, DVDs, fashion magazines, and newspapers as well as make photocopies, fax documents, withdraw money, pay bills, and even mail letters and packages at convenience stores. What's more, you can pick up merchandise, books, and tickets that you order online. During holidays, you can place orders for a festive meal or a cake at a convenience store and then pick it up anytime.

▲ Paying bills

▲ Ticket-buying kiosk

▲ ATM

▲ Salads and noodles

▲ Mailing packages

▲ Hot food

▲ Hotdogs and other foods

照片授權拍攝：統一超商股份有限公司

81

Notes on Pinyin and Pronunciation

1. Pinyin Rules:

When "zh-" , "ch-" , and "sh-" stand alone, an "i" is added to the end. When "-iao" does not follow a consonant, change the "i" to "y" to form yào（要）(see Lesson Three for explanations).

When the vowel "u" is followed by other vowels, but is not preceded by a consonant, change the "u" to "w," as in "u" + "ei" → *wéi*（微）. However, when "u + ei" is preceded by a consonant, the "e" is omitted and the spelling becomes "ui," as in *duì*（對） and *guì*（貴）. The pronunciation, however, remains "du(e)i."

2. Tone Mark Rules (Position of the Tone Marks)

All tone marks in pinyin are placed above the vowels, as in *bà*（爸）, *mā*（媽）, *bó*（伯）, and *mǔ*（母）. Please note that when placing the tone mark above "i," the dot is not necessary, as in *yī*（一）. With compound vowels, the placement of tone marks is prioritized as follows: a > e, o > i, u, ü.

Example

lái（來）, *zhào*（照）, *měi*（美）, *jué*（覺）, *dōu*（都）, *xiǎo*（小）. Also note that a/e, e/o never appear together.

When "i" and "u" appear together, the tone mark is placed above the last appearing vowel, as in *duì*（對）, *niú*（牛）.

Introduction to Chinese Characters

Basic Chinese Radicals

Radicals are components of Chinese characters, usually on the left , that systematically categorize Chinese characters by their meanings. For example, eating " 吃 " and drinking " 喝 " require the use of the mouth, thus they fall under the mouth " 口 " radical; listening " 聽 " requires the use of one's ears, hence naturally belongs to the ear " 耳 " radical. Radicals lend hand to the cognition and memory of Chinese characters, and lead to the understanding of the characters' fundamental meanings. When learners do not know the pronunciation of a certain character, they can use their knowledge of radicals to look up the character. There are 214 radicals in used in modern day dictionaries, below are 35 commonly used ones from words you have already learned thus far.

Chinese Radical	ㄅㄆㄇㄈ	Pinyin	English	Example
人 亻	ㄖㄣ	rén	person	來、你
力	ㄌㄧ	lì	strength	動
口	ㄎㄡ	kǒu	mouth	吃、喝
土	ㄊㄨ	tǔ	earth	坐、塊
夕	ㄒㄧ	xì	sunset	多、外
大	ㄉㄚ	dà	big	天、太
女	ㄋㄩ	nǚ	female	好、姐
子	ㄗ	zǐ	child	學
寸	ㄘㄨㄣ	cùn	inch	對
巾	ㄐㄧㄣ	jīn	napkin	常、幫
心 忄	ㄒㄧㄣ	xīn	heart	想、怡
戈	ㄍㄜ	gē	spear	我
戶	ㄏㄨ	hù	household	房
手 扌	ㄕㄡ	shǒu	hand	打、接
日	ㄖ	rì	sun	明、是
月	ㄩㄝ	yuè	moon	有
木	ㄇㄨ	mù	tree	李、杯
水 氵	ㄕㄨㄟ	shuǐ	water	波、游
火 灬	ㄏㄨㄛ	huǒ	fire	照、熱
玉 王	ㄩ	yù	jade	玩、球
白	ㄅㄞ	bái	white	百、的
目	ㄇㄨ	mù	eye	相、看
竹 竹	ㄓㄨ	zhú	bamboo	籃、網
糸 糸	ㄇㄧ	mì	silk	網
耳	ㄦ	ěr	ear	聽

Chinese Radical	ㄅㄆㄇㄈ	Pinyin	English	Example
肉月	ㄖㄡˋ	ròu	meat	能
見	ㄐㄧㄢˋ	jiàn	see	覺
言	ㄧㄢˊ	yán	speech	請、謝
貝	ㄅㄟˋ	bèi	shell	買、貴
足𧾷	ㄗㄨˊ	zú	foot	踢
走	ㄗㄡˇ	zǒu	walk	起、越
金	ㄐㄧㄣ	jīn	metal	錢
門	ㄇㄣˊ	mén	door	開、關
雨	ㄩˇ	yǔ	rain	電
食飠	ㄕˊ	shí	eat	飯

Self-Assessment Checklist

I can ask and talk about prices.

20%   40%   60%   80%   100%

I can ask for reasons.

20%   40%   60%   80%   100%

I can use simple phrases to describe the size and functions of common objects.

20%   40%   60%   80%   100%

LESSON
5

第五課

牛肉麵真好吃
Beef Noodles Are Really Delicious

學習目標 Learning Objectives

Topic: 飲食 Food and Drink

- Learning the names of common foods and describing their taste.
- Learning to express likes for and make simple comments about food.
- Learning to describe what somebody can/can't do and how well one does it.
- Learning to ask for help.

牛肉麵真好吃

Beef Noodles Are Really Delicious

 對話一 Dialogue 1 　🎧 05-01　AR 05-A

月　美	：	很多人都說臺灣有不少有名的小吃。
Yuèměi	：	Hěn duō rén dōu shuō Táiwān yǒu bù shǎo yǒumíng de xiǎochī.
明　華	：	是啊！牛肉麵、小籠包、臭豆腐…都很好吃。
Mínghuá	：	Shì a! Niúròu miàn, xiǎolóngbāo, chòu dòufǔ...dōu hěn hǎochī.
月　美	：	你最喜歡吃什麼？
Yuèměi	：	Nǐ zuì xǐhuān chī shénme?
明　華	：	牛肉麵。牛肉好吃，湯也好喝。
Mínghuá	：	Niúròu miàn. Niúròu hǎochī, tāng yě hǎohē.
月　美	：	這麼好吃，我很想吃。
Yuèměi	：	Zhème hǎochī, wǒ hěn xiǎng chī.

明　　華 ：我知道一家有名的牛肉麵店，
　　　　　我們一起去吃，怎麼樣？

Mínghuá ：Wǒ zhīdào yì jiā yǒumíng de niúròu miàn diàn, wǒmen yìqǐ qù chī, zěnmeyàng?

月　　美 ：太好了！

Yuèměi ：Tài hǎo le!

明　　華 ：我們明天去。一定要點大碗的。

Mínghuá ：Wǒmen míngtiān qù. Yídìng yào diǎn dà wǎn de.

課文英譯 Text in English

Yuemei ：Many people say Taiwan has quite a few well-known light repasts.

Minghua ：That's right. Beef noodles, xiaolongbao, stinky tofu... are all tasty.

Yuemei ：What do you like to eat most?

Minghua ：Beef noodles. The beef tastes good and the soup is nice.

Yuemei ：That tasty. I would like to have some.

Minghua ：I know a place that is well-known for its beef noodles. Let's go together and have some. What do you say?

Yuemei ：Wonderful!

Minghua ：Let's go tomorrow. You really have to order a large bowl.

生詞一 Vocabulary 1 05-02

Vocabulary

1	牛肉	niúròu	ㄋㄧㄡˊ ㄖㄡˋ	(N)	beef
2	麵	miàn	ㄇㄧㄢˋ	(N)	noodles
3	真	zhēn	ㄓㄣ	(Adv)	really
4	好吃	hǎochī	ㄏㄠˇ ㄔ	(Vs)	delicious
5	說	shuō	ㄕㄨㄛ	(V)	say

6	少	shǎo	ㄕㄠˇ	(Vs-pred)	few in number
7	有名	yǒumíng	ㄧㄡˇ ㄇㄧㄥˊ	(Vs)	well known, famous
8	小吃	xiǎochī	ㄒㄧㄠˇ ㄔ	(N)	light repast, snack
9	最	zuì	ㄗㄨㄟˋ	(Adv)	most
10	湯	tāng	ㄊㄤ	(N)	soup, broth
11	這麼	zhème	ㄓㄜˋ ㄇㄜ	(Adv)	so
12	知道	zhīdào	ㄓ ㄉㄠˋ	(Vst)	to know
13	家	jiā	ㄐㄧㄚ	(M)	measure word for restaurants, shops, etc.
14	店	diàn	ㄉㄧㄢˋ	(N)	shop, store
15	一定	yídìng	ㄧˊ ㄉㄧㄥˋ	(Adv)	really must, definitely
16	點	diǎn	ㄉㄧㄢˇ	(V)	to order (meals)
17	碗	wǎn	ㄨㄢˇ	(M)	a bowl of

Phrases

18	是啊	shì a	ㄕˋ ㄚ˙		That's right.
19	小籠包	xiǎolóngbāo	ㄒㄧㄠˇ ㄌㄨㄥˊ ㄅㄠ		xiaolongbao, e.g., small meat and cabbage-filled steamed buns
20	臭豆腐	chòu dòufǔ	ㄔㄡˋ ㄉㄡˋ ㄈㄨˇ		stinky tofu (fermented tofu)
21	太好了	tài hǎo le	ㄊㄞˋ ㄏㄠˇ ㄌㄜ˙		Excellent. Great.

對話二 Dialogue 2 05-03 05-B

月　美 Yuèměi	：	昨天晚上那家餐廳的菜很好吃， 可是有一點辣。 Zuótiān wǎnshàng nà jiā cāntīng de cài hěn hǎochī, kěshì yǒu yìdiǎn là.
安　同 Āntóng	：	我也怕辣，所以我喜歡自己做飯。 Wǒ yě pà là, suǒyǐ wǒ xǐhuān zìjǐ zuòfàn.
月　美 Yuèměi	：	你做飯做得怎麼樣？ Nǐ zuòfàn zuò de zěnmeyàng?
安　同 Āntóng	：	我做得不好。妳會做飯嗎？ Wǒ zuò de bù hǎo. Nǐ huì zuòfàn ma?
月　美 Yuèměi	：	會。我的甜點也做得不錯。 Huì. Wǒ de tiándiǎn yě zuò de búcuò.
安　同 Āntóng	：	我最喜歡吃甜點。妳可以教我嗎？ Wǒ zuì xǐhuān chī tiándiǎn. Nǐ kěyǐ jiāo wǒ ma?
月　美 Yuèměi	：	好的，這個週末，你到我家來。 Hǎode, zhè ge zhōumò, nǐ dào wǒ jiā lái.
安　同 Āntóng	：	好啊！謝謝妳。 Hǎo a! Xièxie nǐ.

課文英譯 Text in English

Yuemei : The food at the restaurant last night was good, but it was a bit spicy.

Antong : I can't take spicy (food), either. That is why I prefer to cook for myself.

Yuemei : How well do you cook?

Antong : I don't cook well. Can you cook?

Yuemei : Yes. I make good desserts, too.

Antong : I like eating desserts most. Could you teach me?

Yuemei : Sure. Come over to my place this weekend.

Antong : Great! Thank you.

生词二 Vocabulary 2 05-04

Vocabulary

1	昨天	zuótiān	ㄗㄨㄛˊ ㄊㄧㄢ	(N)	yesterday
2	餐廳	cāntīng	ㄘㄢ ㄊㄧㄥ	(N)	restaurant
3	可是	kěshì	ㄎㄜˇ ㄕˋ	(Conj)	but, however
4	辣	là	ㄌㄚˋ	(Vs)	hot (spicy)
5	怕	pà	ㄆㄚˋ	(Vst)	(here) to not like, to fear
6	所以	suǒyǐ	ㄙㄨㄛˇ ㄧˇ	(Conj)	therefore, so
7	自己	zìjǐ	ㄗˋ ㄐㄧˇ	(N)	self
8	做飯	zuòfàn	ㄗㄨㄛˋ ㄈㄢˋ	(V-sep)	to cook
9	得	de	ㄉㄜ˙	(Ptc)	complement marker
10	會	huì	ㄏㄨㄟˋ	(Vaux)	to be able to, can
11	甜點	tiándiǎn	ㄊㄧㄢˊ ㄉㄧㄢˇ	(N)	dessert
12	不錯	búcuò	ㄅㄨˊ ㄘㄨㄛˋ	(Vs)	not bad
13	可以	kěyǐ	ㄎㄜˇ ㄧˇ	(Vaux)	could (possibility)
14	教	jiāo	ㄐㄧㄠ	(V)	to teach
15	到	dào	ㄉㄠˋ	(Prep)	to

Phrases

| 16 | 有一點 | yǒu yìdiǎn | ㄧㄡˇ ㄧˋ ㄉㄧㄢˇ | a little |
| 17 | 不好 | bù hǎo | ㄅㄨˋ ㄏㄠˇ | not well |

文法 Grammar

I. 有一點 yǒu yìdiǎn *slightly* 05-05

Function: 有一點 + State Verb suggests a slightly negative evaluation.

1 這碗牛肉麵有一點辣。
Zhè wǎn niúròu miàn yǒu yìdiǎn là.
This bowl of beef noodle is a little spicy.

2 那支手機有一點貴。
Nà zhī shǒujī yǒu yìdiǎn guì.
That cell phone is a little expensive.

3 他的房子有一點舊。
Tā de fángzi yǒu yìdiǎn jiù.
His house is a little old.

Structures: Since this expression suggests negative evaluation, there is no negative form for the pattern. If the Vs has a positive meaning, it can't be used in this pattern. For example, one can say, 這張照片有一點舊。 Zhè zhāng zhàopiàn yǒu yìdiǎn jiù. 'This photo is a little old'. However, you cannot say *他妹妹有一點漂亮 Tā mèimei yǒu yìdiǎn piàoliàng. 'His younger sister is a little beautiful'.

練習 Exercise

Complete the evaluations.

1 A：你覺得臭豆腐怎麼樣？　B：我覺得臭豆腐 _____ 。

2 A：你覺得那家餐廳的
　　　菜怎麼樣？　　　　　B：那家餐廳的菜 _____ 。

③ A：牛肉麵好吃嗎？　　B：好吃，可是 ＿＿＿＿＿＿＿＿ 。

④ A：那個包子怎麼樣？　　B：好吃，可是我覺得 ＿＿＿＿＿ 。

⑤ A：他的手機是新的嗎？　B：不是新的，＿＿＿＿＿＿＿ 。

II. Complement Marker 得 de 🎧 05-06

Function: The complement marker 得 *de* follows the verb and introduces the complement, which describes the result or state of the action suggested by the verb.

❶ 他學中文學得不錯。
Tā xué Zhōngwén xué de búcuò.
He has learned Chinese quite well.

❷ 王伯母做越南菜做得很好。
Wáng Bómǔ zuò Yuènán cài zuò de hěn hǎo.
Auntie Wang cooks Vietnamese food very well.

❸ 你做得很好。
Nǐ zuò de hěn hǎo.
You did well.

❹ 這種手機賣得很好。
Zhè zhǒng shǒujī mài de hěn hǎo.
This type of cell phone sells well.

Structures: When a complement is added to a transitive verb, several structural consequences follow.

1. When its object directly follows the verb, the verb is repeated before 得 *de* and the complement.

   (1) 你做飯做得真好吃。
   Nǐ zuòfàn zuò de zhēn hǎochī.
   You cook really well.

   (2) 我的老師教中文教得很好。
   Wǒ de lǎoshī jiāo Zhōngwén jiāo de hěn hǎo.
   My teacher teaches Chinese well.

2. When the object appears at the front of the sentence, the verb is not repeated.

   (1) 飯，他做得真好吃。
   Fàn, tā zuò de zhēn hǎochī.
   He cooks really well.

   (2) 中文，你說得很好。
   Zhōngwén, nǐ shuō de hěn hǎo.
   You speak Chinese well.

(3) 這種甜點，他做得很好吃。
Zhè zhǒng tiándiǎn, tā zuò de hěn hǎochī.
He makes this kind of dessert very tasty.

(4) 這支手機賣得很便宜。
Zhè zhī shǒujī mài de hěn piányí.
This cell phone is sold cheaply.

 Negation: Negation occurs only within the complement.

1 他做甜點做得不好。
Tā zuò tiándiǎn zuò de bù hǎo.
He does not make desserts well.

2 王先生打網球打得不好。
Wáng Xiānshēng dǎ wǎngqiú dǎ de bù hǎo.
Mr. Wang does not play the tennis well.

3 他的咖啡賣得不好。
Tā de kāfēi mài de bù hǎo.
His coffee does not sell well.

4 越南菜，這家店做得不好吃。
Yuènán cài, zhè jiā diàn zuò de bù hǎochī.
This shop does not cook Vietnamese food well.

 Questions:

1 他做飯做得怎麼樣？
Tā zuòfàn zuò de zěnmeyàng?
How (well) does he cook?

2 他打籃球打得好嗎？
Tā dǎ lánqiú dǎ de hǎo ma?
Does he play basketball well?

3 中文，他說得好不好？
Zhōngwén, tā shuō de hǎo bù hǎo?
Does he speak Chinese well?

練習 Exercise

Complete the following answers.

1 你弟弟踢足球踢得怎麼樣？　他踢得 ＿＿＿＿＿＿＿＿＿。

2 他姐姐做甜點，做得好吃不好吃？做得 ＿＿＿＿＿＿＿＿＿。

3 日本菜，你妹妹做得好不好？　我妹妹做 ＿＿＿＿＿＿＿。

4 這種手機賣得怎麼樣？　賣得 ＿＿＿＿＿＿＿＿＿。

5 他打網球打得好嗎？　打 ＿＿＿＿＿＿＿＿＿＿。

III. Aquired Skills 會 huì 05-07

Function: 會 *huì* indicates that these skills are acquired through learning.

1 陳小姐會做飯。
Chén Xiǎojiě huì zuòfàn.
Miss Chen can cook.

2 他哥哥會踢足球。
Tā gēge huì tī zúqiú.
His older brother knows how to play soccer.

3 他們兄弟姐妹都會游泳。
Tāmen xiōngdì jiěmèi dōu huì yóuyǒng.
All of those siblings know how to swim.

Structures: 會 *huì* is an auxiliary verb and can be negated.

Negation:

1 他的媽媽不會做飯。
Tā de māma bú huì zuòfàn.
His mom can't cook.

2 我媽媽不會做甜點。
Wǒ māma bú huì zuò tiándiǎn.
My mom does not know how to make desserts.

3 我的家人都不會打棒球。
Wǒ de jiārén dōu bú huì dǎ bàngqiú.
None of the members of my family knows how to play baseball.

Questions:

1 你會做甜點嗎？
Nǐ huì zuò tiándiǎn ma?
Do you know how to make desserts?

2 他弟弟會踢足球嗎？
Tā dìdi huì tī zúqiú ma?
Does his younger brother know how to play football?

3 你會不會說中文？
Nǐ huì bú huì shuō Zhōngwén?
Do you know how to speak Chinese?

4 你的姐姐會不會做飯？
Nǐ de jiějie huì bú huì zuòfàn?
Does your elder sister know how to cook?

練習 Exercise

Complete the answers.

1. A：他會不會做牛肉麵？　　　B：＿＿＿＿，他弟弟也會做。
2. A：你哥哥會不會打網球？　　B：＿＿＿＿，你可以教他嗎？
3. A：我們都會打棒球，你呢？　B：我＿＿＿＿，可是我很想學。
4. A：我會踢足球，你呢？　　　B：我＿＿＿＿，你可以教我嗎？
5. A：小籠包和包子，我都會做，你呢？　B：我也＿＿＿＿。

IV. Destination Marker 到 dào　　🎧 05-08

Function: The preposition 到 *dào* indicates the destination of a movement.

1. 他這個週末到臺灣來。
   Tā zhè ge zhōumò dào Táiwān lái.
   He is coming to Taiwan this weekend.

2. 老師明天到臺北來。我們要和他一起吃晚飯。
   Lǎoshī míngtiān dào Táiběi lái. Wǒmen yào hàn tā yìqǐ chī wǎnfàn.
   The teacher is coming to Taipei tomorrow. We are having dinner with him.

3. 想吃牛肉麵嗎？明天我們可以到那家店去。
   Xiǎng chī niúròu miàn ma? Míngtiān wǒmen kěyǐ dào nà jiā diàn qù.
   Would you like to have beef noodles? We can go to that shop tomorrow.

4. 我可以教你中文，明天到我家來吧！
   Wǒ kěyǐ jiāo nǐ Zhōngwén, míngtiān dào wǒ jiā lái ba!
   I can teach you Chinese. Go ahead and come to my house tomorrow.

Structures:

Negation: Negation is always done by placing a negator in front of a preposition, not the main verb.

① 王先生明天不到臺北來。

Wáng Xiānshēng míngtiān bú dào Táiběi lái.

Mr. Wang is not coming to Taipei tomorrow.

② 那家的越南菜不好吃。他們不到那家餐廳去。

Nà jiā de Yuènán cài bù hǎochī. Tāmen bú dào nà jiā cāntīng qù.

That shop's Vietnamese food doesn't taste good. They don't go to that restaurant.

③ 他晚上去看電影，不到我家來，你呢？

Tā wǎnshàng qù kàn diànyǐng, bú dào wǒ jiā lái, nǐ ne?

He is going to go to a movie tonight and will not be coming to my house. How about you?

Questions: 到 *dào* can be used to form A-not-A questions.

① 你妹妹到不到臺灣來？

Nǐ mèimei dào bú dào Táiwān lái?

Is your younger sister coming to Taiwan?

② 他們到不到我家來？

Tāmen dào bú dào wǒ jiā lái?

Are they coming to my house?

Usage: The destination marker 到 *dào* is a preposition and another verb serves as the main verb in the sentence（e.g., 來 *lái* 'come' or 去 *qù* 'go'). In Taiwan and Southern China, however, 到 *dào* is often used as a verb, like 來 *lái* or 去 *qù* .

① 這麼多家餐廳，我們要到哪一家？

Zhème duō jiā cāntīng, wǒmen yào dào nǎ yì jiā?

There are so many restaurants. Which one should we go?

② 他們明天晚上要到王老師家。你想去嗎？

Tāmen míngtiān wǎnshàng yào dào Wáng lǎoshī jiā. Nǐ xiǎng qù ma?

They are going to Teacher Wang's house tomorrow evening. Would you like to go?

3 歡迎你到我家。

Huānyíng nǐ dào wǒ jiā.

Welcome to my home.

練習 Exercise

Make correct sentences by rearranging the order of the characters (1-3) or complete the sentences by filling in the blanks (4-5).

1 臺北　陳小姐　到　來
　　①　　　②　　　③　④

　　_____。

2 不到　來　臺灣　李先生
　　①　　②　　③　　　④

　　_____。

3 到不到　週末　老師　臺北　來
　　①　　　②　　　③　　④　　⑤

　　_____？

4 那兩個日本人 _____ 臺灣 _____。

5 李先生要去打球，他不 _____ 我家 _____。

課 室 活 動 **Classroom Activities**

I. Street Vendor Food Is Good

Goal: Learning the names of common foods and how to read them.

Task: Compete with classmates to see who can name the most street foods. Find pictures of food you know and bring them to class. Show each picture and say the name of the food it shows.

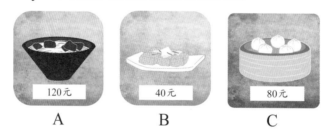

120元   40元   80元

A   B   C

臭豆腐 _____   小籠包 _____   牛肉麵 _____

II. Tell Us What You Think

Goal: Learning to make simple comments about common objects.

Task: Read the following statements, then make comments on the statements using 很, 太 or 有一點.

Example

A：一碗牛肉麵一百八十塊錢。
Yì wǎn niúròu miàn yìbǎi bāshí kuài qián.
A bowl of beef noodles costs NT$180.

B：有一點貴。
Yǒu yìdiǎn guì.
A bit expensive.

❶ 十個小籠包一百六十塊。→ _____。

❷ 四個甜點一百塊。 → _____。

❸ 一杯咖啡十五塊。 → _____。

❹ 一支手機兩萬多。 → _____。

❺ → _____。

III. Talent Contest

Goal: Learning to describe what someone can/can't do and how well s/he does it.

Task: There is going to be a talent contest at school. Find out what your classmates can do and how well they can do it. Record your findings. Ask questions using phrases that you learned, like 做甜點、游泳、照相、打籃球、踢足球、做小籠包、打網球 . (Make desserts, swim, take pictures, play basketball, play soccer, make xiaolongbao, play tennis.)

問題 Question	回答 Answer	問題 Question	結果 Finding
你會做飯嗎？ 你會不會做飯？	☐會 ☐不會	你做得 怎麼樣？	1. _____會做飯，做得很好。 2. _____不會做飯。 3. _____會做飯，可是做得不好。

IV. Asking for Help

Goal: Learning to ask for help.

Task: From the survey you completed in Task III, find one item that interests you and ask the person if s/he could teach you how do to it, e.g., 我想學做小籠包，你可以教我嗎？ (I want to learn how to make xiaolongbao. Can you teach me?)

文化 *Bits of Chinese Culture*

Queuing up at Food Stands

Lines in front of roadside food stands are a familiar scene in Taiwan. Food stalls usually open for business at fixed times and in fixed locations. As long as the food sold at a stall is fresh, inexpensive, and good, you can be sure there will be a long queue in front of it regardless of the weather.

▲ Lines in front of popular roadside food stands

With a little pocket change, you can buy delicious baozi, scallion pancakes, wheel-barrel cakes, or pan-fried dumplings. It is little wonder that there are queues on almost every street corner.

Street Vendors in Taiwan

Street vendors are very common in Taiwan. They are the product of farmer's markets and temple festivals of an agricultural society of a time passed. Today, street vendors are seen in scenic sites, residential areas, outskirts of markets, business district surroundings, on arcaded corridors, on the streets, outside examination sites, and during temple festivals. The selections of vendors range from daily goods to food to souvenirs. Since street vendors are very mobile, they sometimes affect traffic, disturb quiet neighborhoods, or scar cityscape. If street vendors could be regulated, they could add to the excitement and beauty of the city.

▲ Street vendors at scenic sites

Notes on Pinyin and Pronunciation

Pinyin Rules

As with "zh-/zhi," "ch-/chi," and "sh-/shi," when "z-," "c-," and "s-" stand alone, "i" is added to form zi, ci, and si.

When "u" is followed by other vowels, but is not preceded by a consonant, change the "u" to "w," as in "u" + "ei" → wéi 微 in Lesson Four and "u" + "o" → wǒ 我 in Lesson 1.

When the vowel "i" is followed by "ou" but is not preceded by a consonant, change the "i" to "y" to form 有 yǒu (Refer to Lesson 2). When a consonant precedes the "i" + "ou" compound, the "o" is omitted and it becomes "-iu," e.g., 牛 → niú, 六 → liù. The "o," however, is still pronounced, e.g., → "ni(o)ú" and "li(o)ù."

Introduction to Chinese Characters
The Earliest Chinese Characters

There are three general beliefs regarding the origin of Chinese characters:

1. Chinese characters were created by a person by the name of Cangjie.

2. Chinese characters originated from the eight trigrams and rope-knotting.

3. Chinese characters originated from pictograms. This is also the most widely adopted belief among scholars.

Characters were not created by any single person, at any single time, or at any specific place. They were developed and accumulated over time. Most scholars believe that Chinese characters originated from pictures or drawings and slowly became signs and characters.

The Chinese characters we see and use today have undergone many thousands of years of evolution, from the oracle bone script of the Shang Dynasty to bronze script and Large Seal script of the Zhou Dynasty to the Small Seal script that was adopted after the Qin Dynasty and used to unite the Six Kingdoms. These scripts are classified as ancient scripts. During the Han Dynasty, the symmetrical and rounded look of Small Seal script was modified to become more rectangular and orderly, making writing easier and faster. This came to known as Clerical script. The Regular script we use now evolved directly from the Clerical script. In other words, the standardized characters in use today were shaped and formed during the Han Dynasty.

甲骨文 Shang Dynasty (circa 1776-1122 B.C.)	金文 Zhou Dynasty (circa 1122-249 B.C.)	小篆 Qin Dynasty (circa 221-206 B.C.)	隸書 Han Dynasty (circa 200 B.C.)	楷書 Han Dynasty (circa 200 B.C.)
毋	毋	毋	女	女

Self-Assessment Checklist

I know the names of some common foods and can describe their taste.

20%   40%   60%   80%   100%

I can express food preferences and make simple comments about them.

20%   40%   60%   80%   100%

I can describe what others can/can't do and how well they do it.

20%   40%   60%   80%   100%

I can ask for help.

20%   40%   60%   80%   100%

Pinyin	Traditional Characters	Simplified Characters	Lesson-Dialogue-Number
A			
a	啊	啊	3-1-21
a	啊	啊	13-1-4
ǎi	矮	矮	10-2-9
B			
ba	吧	吧	3-2-9
ba	吧	吧	10-1-10
bǎ	把	把	15-1-17
bàba	爸爸	爸爸	2-1-20
bǎi	百	百	4-1-15
Bái Rúyù	白如玉	白如玉	3-2-1
bàn	半	半	7-2-6
bāng	幫	帮	4-1-13
bàngqiú	棒球	棒球	3-1-7
bāo	包	包	15-2-16
bǎoxiǎn	保險	保险	15-2-10
bāozi	包子	包子	4-1-8
bēi	杯	杯	4-1-6
bǐ	比	比	8-2-8
biànlì shāngdiàn	便利商店	便利商店	8-1-20
bié	別	別	15-2-14
bǐjiào	比較	比较	8-1-8
bīng	冰	冰	15-2-13
bǐsài	比賽	比赛	7-2-7
bíshuǐ	鼻水	鼻水	15-1-4
bómǔ	伯母	伯母	2-2-2
bù	不	不	1-2-11
bù hǎo	不好	不好	5-2-17
bù xíng	不行	不行	8-2-12
búbì kèqì	不必客氣	不必客气	13-1-22
búcuò	不錯	不错	5-2-12
búguò	不過	不过	11-2-12
bùhǎo yìsi	不好意思	不好意思	11-2-15
búkèqì	不客氣	不客气	1-1-22

Pinyin	Traditional Characters	Simplified Characters	Lesson-Dialogue-Number
búyòng le	不用了	不用了	15-2-20
C			
cài	菜	菜	3-2-16
cānguān	參觀	参观	8-2-2
cāntīng	餐廳	餐厅	5-2-2
chá	茶	茶	1-2-3
chā	差	差	15-1-8
chābùduō	差不多	差不多	8-2-14
cháguǎn	茶館	茶馆	9-2-12
cháng	常	常	3-1-10
chànggē	唱歌	唱歌	7-1-3
chāoshì	超市	超市	11-1-8
Chén Yuèměi	陳月美	陈月美	1-1-1
chéngjī	成績	成绩	12-1-11
chēpiào	車票	车票	8-1-10
chī	吃	吃	3-2-14
chīchīkàn	吃吃看	吃吃看	10-1-15
chīfàn	吃飯	吃饭	6-2-10
chòu dòufǔ	臭豆腐	臭豆腐	5-1-20
chuān	穿	穿	10-2-4
chuānghù	窗戶	窗户	10-2-13
chuántǒng	傳統	传统	13-2-9
chúfáng	廚房	厨房	11-1-4
chūntiān	春天	春天	14-1-5
chūqù	出去	出去	9-1-8
cì	次	次	15-2-6
cóng	從	从	7-1-6
D			
dà	大	大	4-1-10
dǎ	打	打	3-1-5
dà bùfèn	大部分	大部分	13-2-15
dǎ diànhuà	打電話	打电话	11-1-23
Dà'ān	大安	大安	7-1-12
dàgài	大概	大概	9-1-9

Pinyin	Traditional Characters	Simplified Characters	Lesson-Dialogue-Number
dài	帶	带	9-2-4
dàjiā	大家	大家	14-2-10
dàlóu	大樓	大楼	6-2-14
dàn	蛋	蛋	13-2-7
dàngāo	蛋糕	蛋糕	13-2-11
dāngrán	當然	当然	13-1-8
dànshì	但是	但是	8-1-12
dào	到	到	5-2-15
dào	到	到	11-1-12
dào	到	到	12-1-17
dǎsuàn	打算	打算	9-1-3
dàxué	大學	大学	12-1-7
de	的	的	2-1-3
de	得	得	5-2-9
děi	得	得	7-1-8
děng	等	等	11-2-9
děng yíxià	等一下	等一下	7-2-20
diàn	店	店	5-1-14
diǎn	點	点	5-1-16
diǎn	點	点	7-1-1
diànhuà	電話	电话	11-1-20
diànshì	電視	电视	9-1-4
diànyǐng	電影	电影	3-2-5
dìdi	弟弟	弟弟	10-2-11
dìfāng	地方	地方	6-1-15
dìng	訂	订	13-2-3
dòng	棟	栋	6-2-13
dōngtiān	冬天	冬天	14-1-10
dōngxi	東西	东西	6-2-6
dōu	都	都	2-1-13
duì	對	对	10-1-11
duì	對	对	13-2-12
duìbùqǐ	對不起	对不起	1-2-18
duìle	對了	对了	7-1-15
duō	多	多	2-1-11
duō jiǔ	多久	多久	9-1-13
duōshǎo	多少	多少	4-1-2
dùzi	肚子	肚子	15-2-3

Pinyin	Traditional Characters	Simplified Characters	Lesson-Dialogue-Number
F			
fāngbiàn	方便	方便	6-2-2
fángdōng	房東	房东	11-1-2
fàngjià	放假	放假	9-1-10
fángjiān	房間	房间	11-1-15
fángzi	房子	房子	2-1-7
fángzū	房租	房租	11-2-2
fāshāo	發燒	发烧	15-1-12
fāyán	發炎	发炎	15-1-10
fēicháng	非常	非常	8-1-11
fēn	分	分	7-1-4
fēng	風	风	14-1-3
fēngjǐng	風景	风景	6-1-8
fēnzhōng	分鐘	分钟	11-1-10
fù	付	付	11-2-13
fùjìn	附近	附近	6-1-17
fùmǔ	父母	父母	14-1-9
G			
gāng	剛	刚	7-2-3
gānjìng	乾淨	干净	10-2-12
gǎnmào	感冒	感冒	15-1-13
gāo	高	高	10-2-10
gāotiě	高鐵	高铁	8-1-18
ge	個	个	2-2-10
gēge	哥哥	哥哥	2-2-6
gěi	給	给	10-1-4
gěi	給	给	11-1-21
gēn	跟	跟	8-1-3
gēn	跟	跟	15-2-11
gèng	更	更	14-2-9
gōnggòng qìchē	公共汽車（公車）	公共汽车（公车）	8-2-11
gōngkè	功課	功课	9-1-7
gōngsī	公司	公司	12-1-13
gōngzuò	工作	工作	12-2-1
gōngzuò	工作	工作	12-2-8
guàng	逛	逛	9-2-10

Pinyin	Traditional Characters	Simplified Characters	Lesson-Dialogue-Number
guānxīn	關心	关心	15-2-15
gǔdài	古代	古代	8-2-3
Gùgōng Bówùyuàn	故宮博物院（故宮）	故宫博物院（故宫）	8-2-9
guì	貴	贵	4-2-11
guò	過	过	13-1-15
guójiā	國家	国家	12-2-10

H

Pinyin	Traditional Characters	Simplified Characters	Lesson-Dialogue-Number
hái	還	还	9-2-6
hǎi	海	海	6-1-11
háishì	還是	还是	3-2-8
hàn	和	和	3-1-8
hào	號	号	9-2-3
hǎo	好	好	1-1-14
hǎo	好	好	2-1-9
hǎo	好	好	12-2-6
hǎo a	好啊	好啊	3-1-23
hǎo bù hǎo	好不好	好不好	3-2-18
hǎochī	好吃	好吃	5-1-4
hǎode	好的	好的	4-1-17
hǎohē	好喝	好喝	1-2-5
hǎojiǔ bújiàn	好久不見	好久不见	13-1-21
hǎokàn	好看	好看	2-1-16
hǎowán	好玩	好玩	3-1-16
hǎoxiàng	好像	好像	11-2-7
hē	喝	喝	1-2-2
hěn	很	很	1-2-4
hóngsè	紅色	红色	10-1-8
hóngyè	紅葉	红叶	14-1-13
hóulóng	喉嚨	喉咙	15-1-9
hòumiàn	後面	后面	6-1-12
hòutiān	後天	后天	7-1-11
huā	花	花	12-1-9
Huālián	花蓮	花莲	6-1-22
huángsè	黃色	黄色	10-1-2
huānyíng	歡迎	欢迎	1-1-19
huáxuě	滑雪	滑雪	14-1-4
huì	會	会	5-2-10

Pinyin	Traditional Characters	Simplified Characters	Lesson-Dialogue-Number
huì	會	会	11-2-8
huí jiā	回家	回家	15-2-22
huíguó	回國	回国	9-1-2
huílái	回來	回来	13-1-3
huíqù	回去	回去	11-1-17
huǒchē	火車	火车	8-1-2
huòshì	或是	或是	8-1-16

J

Pinyin	Traditional Characters	Simplified Characters	Lesson-Dialogue-Number
jǐ	幾	几	2-2-9
jǐ	幾	几	15-2-5
jiā	家	家	2-1-5
jiā	家	家	5-1-13
jiān	間	间	11-1-13
jiǎngxuéjīn	獎學金	奖学金	12-1-10
jiànkāng	健康	健康	15-2-9
jiànkāng zhōngxīn	健康中心	健康中心	15-2-21
jiànmiàn	見面	见面	7-1-5
jiànyì	建議	建议	9-2-7
jiào	叫	叫	1-1-16
jiāo	教	教	5-2-14
jiāohuàn	交換	交换	13-1-10
jiàoshì	教室	教室	6-2-17
jiārén	家人	家人	2-1-4
jiāyóu	加油	加油	12-1-22
jīchē	機車	机车	8-2-5
jìchéngchē	計程車	计程车	8-2-13
jìde	記得	记得	13-1-7
jiē	接	接	1-1-9
jiějie	姐姐	姐姐	2-1-18
jiěmèi	姐妹	姐妹	2-2-13
jiéshù	結束	结束	7-2-8
jiéyùn	捷運	捷运	8-2-7
jìhuà	計畫	计画	12-1-1
jīhuì	機會	机会	10-1-13
jìn	近	近	6-2-1
jīnnián	今年	今年	13-2-2
jīntiān	今天	今天	3-2-2

Pinyin	Traditional Characters	Simplified Characters	Lesson-Dialogue-Number
jiù	舊	旧	4-2-5
jiù	就	就	9-2-15
jiù	就	就	11-1-11
jiǔ	久	久	12-1-3
juéde	覺得	觉得	3-1-15
juédìng	決定	决定	9-2-13

K

Pinyin	Traditional Characters	Simplified Characters	Lesson-Dialogue-Number
kāfēi	咖啡	咖啡	1-2-14
kāishǐ	開始	开始	7-2-15
kāixīn	開心	开心	10-2-3
kàn	看	看	3-2-4
kànbìng	看病	看病	15-2-8
kànshū	看書	看书	2-2-8
kè	課	课	7-2-14
kěpà	可怕	可怕	14-2-12
kěshì	可是	可是	5-2-3
kètīng	客廳	客厅	11-1-3
kěyǐ	可以	可以	3-2-10
kěyǐ	可以	可以	5-2-13
kěyǐ	可以	可以	7-2-18
kōng	空	空	11-1-14
kuài	塊	块	4-1-16
kuài	塊	块	10-1-5
kuài	快	块	8-1-9
kuài	快	快	14-1-8
kuàilè	快樂	快乐	13-1-2
KTV	KTV	KTV	7-1-2

L

Pinyin	Traditional Characters	Simplified Characters	Lesson-Dialogue-Number
là	辣	辣	5-2-4
lái	來	来	1-1-5
lánqiú	籃球	篮球	3-1-11
lánsè	藍色	蓝色	10-2-15
lǎobǎn	老闆	老板	4-1-4
lǎoshī	老師	老师	2-2-7
le	了	了	4-2-6
le	了	了	13-2-4
lèi	累	累	12-1-20
lěng	冷	冷	14-1-2

Pinyin	Traditional Characters	Simplified Characters	Lesson-Dialogue-Number
Lǐ Mínghuá	李明華	李明华	1-1-2
liǎng	兩	两	2-2-15
liǎnsè	臉色	脸色	15-2-1
lǐmiàn	裡面	里面	6-2-8
Lín	林	林	11-1-22
liú	流	流	15-1-3
lǐwù	禮物	礼物	13-2-1
lóu	樓	楼	6-2-12
lóuxià	樓下	楼下	6-1-18
lǚguǎn	旅館	旅馆	10-2-6
lǚxíng	旅行	旅行	9-1-6

M

Pinyin	Traditional Characters	Simplified Characters	Lesson-Dialogue-Number
ma	嗎	吗	1-1-8
Mǎ Āntóng	馬安同	马安同	2-1-2
mài	賣	卖	4-2-12
mǎi	買	买	4-1-5
māma	媽媽	妈妈	2-1-21
màn	慢	慢	8-1-6
màn zǒu	慢走	慢走	14-2-17
máng	忙	忙	7-2-10
mángguǒ	芒果	芒果	10-1-3
Māokōng	貓空	猫空	9-2-16
méi	沒	没	2-2-11
měi	美	美	6-1-9
měi	每	每	7-2-11
méi guānxi	沒關係	没关系	11-2-16
méi wèntí	沒問題	没问题	7-1-14
Měiguó	美國	美国	1-2-17
mèimei	妹妹	妹妹	2-1-19
ménkǒu	門口	门口	13-1-17
miàn	麵	面	5-1-2
miànxiàn	麵線	面线	13-2-6
míngnián	明年	明年	14-1-11
míngtiān	明天	明天	3-1-17
míngzi	名字	名字	2-2-4

N

Pinyin	Traditional Characters	Simplified Characters	Lesson-Dialogue-Number
ná	拿	拿	15-1-16
nà	那	那	11-2-10

Pinyin	Traditional Characters	Simplified Characters	Lesson-Dialogue-Number
nà / nèi	那	那	4-2-10
nǎ / něi	哪	哪	1-2-12
nǎ guó / něi guó	哪國	哪国	1-2-19
nàlǐ	那裡	那里	6-1-7
nǎlǐ	哪裡	哪里	6-1-5
Nǎlǐ, nǎlǐ	哪裡，哪裡	哪里，哪里	13-2-14
nàme	那麼	那么	12-2-13
nàme	那麼	那么	13-1-11
nán	男	男	10-2-8
nán	難	难	12-2-12
nánkàn	難看	难看	15-2-2
ne	呢	呢	1-2-9
nèiyòng	內用	内用	4-1-19
néng	能	能	4-2-8
nǐ	你	你	1-1-4
nǐ	妳	妳	3-2-6
nǐ hǎo	你好	你好	1-1-23
nián	年	年	12-1-2
niàn	念	念	12-1-6
niánqīng	年輕	年轻	13-2-10
niànshū	念書	念书	12-1-19
nǐmen	你們	你们	1-1-17
nín	您	您	2-2-3
niúròu	牛肉	牛肉	5-1-1
Niǔyuē	紐約	纽约	14-1-16
nǚ	女	女	9-2-1

P

Pinyin	Traditional Characters	Simplified Characters	Lesson-Dialogue-Number
pà	怕	怕	5-2-5
pāi	拍	拍	10-2-1
pángbiān	旁邊	旁边	6-2-16
péi	陪	陪	15-2-7
péngyǒu	朋友	朋友	6-1-20
piányí	便宜	便宜	4-2-13
piàoliàng	漂亮	漂亮	2-1-6

Q

Pinyin	Traditional Characters	Simplified Characters	Lesson-Dialogue-Number
qí	騎	骑	8-2-4
qián	錢	钱	4-1-3
qiān	千	千	4-2-16

Pinyin	Traditional Characters	Simplified Characters	Lesson-Dialogue-Number
qiánmiàn	前面	前面	6-1-10
qǐng	請	请	1-2-1
qǐng	請	请	10-1-14
qǐng jìn	請進	请进	2-1-22
qǐngwèn	請問	请问	1-1-20
qiūtiān	秋天	秋天	14-1-12
qù	去	去	3-1-19
qùnián	去年	去年	12-2-2

R

Pinyin	Traditional Characters	Simplified Characters	Lesson-Dialogue-Number
rè	熱	热	4-1-7
rén	人	人	1-2-7
rèshuǐqì	熱水器	热水器	11-2-6
rèxīn	熱心	热心	13-1-12
Rìběn	日本	日本	1-2-16

S

Pinyin	Traditional Characters	Simplified Characters	Lesson-Dialogue-Number
sǎn	傘	伞	14-2-2
shān	山	山	6-1-13
shàng cì	上次	上次	14-2-16
shàng ge yuè	上個月	上个月	10-2-18
shàngbān	上班	上班	12-1-18
shāngdiàn	商店	商店	6-2-9
shàngkè	上課	上课	6-1-21
shàngwǎng	上網	上网	4-2-9
shānshàng	山上	山上	6-1-4
shǎo	少	少	5-1-6
shéi	誰	谁	2-1-17
shēngbìng	生病	生病	15-1-11
shēngrì	生日	生日	13-1-1
shēngrì kuàilè	生日快樂	生日快乐	13-1-19
shēngyì	生意	生意	12-2-4
shénme	什麼	什么	1-2-6
shì	是	是	1-1-6
shì	試	试	12-2-11
shī	濕	湿	14-2-6
shì a	是啊	是啊	5-1-18
shí'èryuè dǐ	十二月底	十二月底	14-1-18
shìde	是的	是的	1-1-21
shíhòu	時候	时候	7-1-10

Pinyin	Traditional Characters	Simplified Characters	Lesson-Dialogue-Number
shíjiān	時間	时间	12-1-4
shìshìkàn	試試看	试试看	12-2-15
shōudào	收到	收到	11-2-14
shǒujī	手機	手机	4-2-3
shū	書	书	2-2-5
shūfǎ	書法	书法	7-2-13
shūfú	舒服	舒服	8-1-14
shuì	睡	睡	15-2-17
shuǐ	水	水	15-1-18
shuǐguǒ	水果	水果	10-1-1
shuìjiào	睡覺	睡觉	15-1-20
shuō	說	说	5-1-5
suǒyǐ	所以	所以	5-2-6
sùshè	宿舍	宿舍	6-2-11

T

Pinyin	Traditional Characters	Simplified Characters	Lesson-Dialogue-Number
tā	他	他	1-2-10
tā	她	她	9-2-5
tài	太	太	4-2-4
tài hǎo le	太好了	太好了	5-1-21
tài kèqì	太客氣	太客气	13-1-23
Táidōng	臺東	台东	9-1-14
táifēng	颱風	台风	14-2-3
Táinán	臺南	台南	8-1-17
tàitai	太太	太太	10-2-7
Táiwān	臺灣（＝台灣）	台湾（＝台湾）	1-1-18
tāmen	他們	他们	6-1-1
tāng	湯	汤	5-1-10
tàofáng	套房	套房	11-1-16
tǎoyàn	討厭	讨厌	14-2-7
tèbié	特別	特别	9-2-11
tì	替	替	12-1-14
tī	踢	踢	3-1-13
tián	甜	甜	10-1-7
tiān	天	天	7-2-12
tiándiǎn	甜點	甜点	5-2-11
tiānqì	天氣	天气	14-1-1
Tiánzhōng Chéngyī	田中誠一	田中诚一	2-2-1

Pinyin	Traditional Characters	Simplified Characters	Lesson-Dialogue-Number
tíng	停	停	14-2-13
tīng	聽	听	3-1-2
tīngshuō	聽說	听说	6-1-23
tòng	痛	痛	15-1-6
tóngxué	同學	同学	8-2-1
tóu	頭	头	15-1-5
tù	吐	吐	15-2-4
túshūguǎn	圖書館	图书馆	6-2-15

W

Pinyin	Traditional Characters	Simplified Characters	Lesson-Dialogue-Number
wàidài	外帶	外带	4-1-18
wàimiàn	外面	外面	6-2-7
wán	玩	玩	8-1-4
wàn	萬	万	4-2-15
wǎn	碗	碗	5-1-17
wǎnfàn	晚飯	晚饭	3-2-15
wǎng	往	往	10-2-14
Wáng Kāiwén	王開文	王开文	1-1-3
wàngle	忘（了）	忘（了）	13-1-6
wǎnglù shàng	網路上	网路上	8-1-19
wǎngqiú	網球	网球	3-1-6
wǎnshàng	晚上	晚上	3-2-3
wànshì rúyì	萬事如意	万事如意	13-2-16
wéi	喂	喂	11-2-1
wéibō	微波	微波	4-1-14
wèikǒu	胃口	胃口	15-1-7
wèishénme	為什麼	为什么	4-2-17
wèn	問	问	7-2-19
wèntí	問題	问题	11-2-5
wǒ	我	我	1-1-11
wǒ jiù shì	我就是	我就是	13-1-20
wǒmen	我們	我们	1-1-10
wǔ	五	五	2-2-14
wǔcān	午餐	午餐	7-2-2
Wūlóng chá	烏龍茶	乌龙茶	1-2-15

X

Pinyin	Traditional Characters	Simplified Characters	Lesson-Dialogue-Number
xià cì	下次	下次	7-1-13
xià ge xīngqí	下個星期	下个星期	9-1-11
xiàkè	下課	下课	7-2-4

Pinyin	Traditional Characters	Simplified Characters	Lesson-Dialogue-Number
xiān	先	先	12-1-5
xiǎng	想	想	3-2-7
xiǎng	想	想	11-1-18
xiǎng	想	想	14-1-6
xiāng	香	香	10-1-6
xiānshēng	先生	先生	1-1-13
xiànzài	現在	现在	6-1-16
xiào	笑	笑	10-2-2
xiǎo	小	小	4-1-12
xiǎochī	小吃	小吃	5-1-8
xiǎojiě	小姐	小姐	1-1-7
xiǎolóngbāo	小籠包	小笼包	5-1-19
xiǎoshí	小時	小时	15-2-18
xiǎoxīn	小心	小心	14-2-11
xiàtiān	夏天	夏天	14-2-5
xiàwǔ	下午	下午	7-2-5
xiàxuě	下雪	下雪	14-1-17
xiàyǔ	下雨	下雨	14-2-14
Xībānyá	西班牙	西班牙	13-1-18
Xībānyá wén	西班牙文	西班牙文	13-1-13
xiě	寫	写	7-2-17
xièxie	謝謝	谢谢	1-1-22
xīguā	西瓜	西瓜	10-1-9
xíguàn	習慣	习惯	11-2-4
xǐhuān	喜歡	喜欢	1-2-8
xīn	新	新	4-2-2
xìng	姓	姓	1-1-15
xīngqí	星期	星期	9-1-1
xīnnián	新年	新年	14-1-7
xīnwén	新聞	新闻	14-2-8
xīnxiǎng shìchéng	心想事成	心想事成	13-2-17
xiōngdì	兄弟	兄弟	2-2-12
xiūxí	休息	休息	15-1-19
xīwàng	希望	希望	12-1-15
xué	學	学	3-2-11
xuéfèi	學費	学费	12-1-12
xuéshēng	學生	学生	6-2-4

Pinyin	Traditional Characters	Simplified Characters	Lesson-Dialogue-Number
xuéxiào	學校	学校	6-1-2
xūyào	需要	需要	12-1-8
Y			
yào	要	要	1-2-13
yào	要	要	4-1-9
yào	要	要	4-2-14
yào	要	要	14-2-4
yào	藥	药	15-1-14
yàojú	藥局	药局	15-1-15
yàoshì	要是	要是	9-2-14
yě	也	也	3-1-12
yèshì	夜市	夜市	9-2-8
yìdiǎn	一點	一点	13-2-8
yídìng	一定	一定	5-1-15
yīfú	衣服	衣服	10-2-5
yígòng	一共	一共	4-1-1
yǐhòu	以後	以后	12-1-16
yǐhòu	以後	以后	12-2-5
yǐjīng	已經	已经	11-2-3
yīnggāi	應該	应该	9-2-9
yǐngpiàn	影片	影片	9-1-5
yínháng	銀行	银行	7-1-9
yīnwèi	因為	因为	10-2-16
yīnyuè	音樂	音乐	3-1-3
yìqǐ	一起	一起	3-2-13
yǐqián	以前	以前	10-1-12
yīshēng	醫生	医生	15-1-1
yíyàng	一樣	一样	13-1-14
yìzhí	一直	一直	15-1-2
yóu	油	油	15-2-12
yòu	又	又	8-1-13
yǒu	有	有	2-1-10
yǒu kòng	有空	有空	7-1-16
yǒu shì	有事	有事	7-2-21
yǒu shíhòu	有時候	有时候	9-1-12
yǒu yìdiǎn	有一點	有一点	5-2-16
yǒu yìsi	有意思	有意思	7-2-22

Pinyin	Traditional Characters	Simplified Characters	Lesson-Dialogue-Number
yòubiān	右邊	右边	11-1-6
yǒumíng	有名	有名	5-1-7
yǒuxiàn diànshì	有線電視	有线电视	11-2-17
yóuyǒng	游泳	游泳	3-1-9
yóuyǒngchí	游泳池	游泳池	6-2-18
yǔ	雨	雨	14-2-1
yuǎn	遠	远	6-1-6
yuè	月	月	9-2-2
Yuènán	越南	越南	3-2-17
yùndòng	運動	运动	3-1-4
Yùshān	玉山	玉山	14-1-15
yùshì	浴室	浴室	11-1-7
yǔyán	語言	语言	13-1-9
yǔyán zhōngxīn	語言中心	语言中心	12-1-21

Z

Pinyin	Traditional Characters	Simplified Characters	Lesson-Dialogue-Number
zài	在	在	6-1-3
zài	在	在	6-2-5
zài	在	在	7-2-1
zài	載	载	8-2-6
zài	再	再	11-1-19
zài	再	再	12-2-14
zàijiàn	再見	再见	7-1-17
zǎo yìdiǎn	早一點	早一点	15-1-21
zǎoshàng	早上	早上	3-1-18
zěnme	怎麼	怎么	8-1-5
zěnme	怎麼	怎么	13-1-5
zěnme le	怎麼了	怎么了	15-2-19
zěnmeyàng	怎麼樣	怎么样	3-1-20
zhàn	站	站	8-1-15
zhāng	張	张	2-1-15
Zhāng Yíjūn	張怡君	张怡君	2-1-1
zhǎo	找	找	6-1-19
zhǎo	找	找	12-2-7
zhàopiàn	照片	照片	2-1-12
zhàoxiàng	照相	照相	2-1-14
zhè / zhèi	這	这	1-1-12
zhè cì	這次	这次	14-2-15
zhèlǐ	這裡	这里	6-2-3
zhème	這麼	这么	5-1-11

Pinyin	Traditional Characters	Simplified Characters	Lesson-Dialogue-Number
zhēn	真	真	5-1-3
zhēnde	真的	真的	6-1-14
zhèxiē	這些	这些	10-2-19
zhèyàng	這樣	这样	12-2-9
zhǐ	只	只	14-1-14
zhī	支	支	4-2-1
zhīdào	知道	知道	5-1-12
zhǒng	種	种	4-2-7
zhōng	中	中	4-1-11
Zhōngguó	中國	中国	8-2-10
zhōngtóu	鐘頭	钟头	8-1-7
Zhōngwén	中文	中文	3-2-12
zhōngwǔ	中午	中午	7-1-7
zhōumò	週末	周末	3-1-1
zhù	住	住	10-2-17
zhù	祝	祝	13-2-13
zhuāng	裝	装	11-2-11
zhūjiǎo	豬脚	猪脚	13-2-5
zì	字	字	7-2-16
zìjǐ	自己	自己	5-2-7
zǒulù	走路	走路	11-1-9
zū	租	租	11-1-1
zuì	最	最	5-1-9
zuìhǎo	最好	最好	15-2-23
zuìjìn	最近	最近	7-2-9
zuò	坐	坐	2-1-8
zuò	坐	坐	8-1-1
zuò	做	做	12-2-3
zuò shénme	做什麼	做什么	3-1-22
zuǒbiān	左邊	左边	11-1-5
zuòfàn	做飯	做饭	5-2-8
zuótiān	昨天	昨天	5-2-1
zuǒyòu	左右	左右	13-1-16
zúqiú	足球	足球	3-1-14

English definition	Traditional Characters	Simplified Characters	Lesson-Dialogue-Number
A			
a bit earlier	早一點	早一点	15-1-21
(a) few	幾	几	15-2-5
a little	有一點	有一点	5-2-16
a little, some	一點	一点	13-2-8
about the same	差不多	差不多	8-2-14
to access the internet, to use the internet	上網	上网	4-2-9
afternoon	下午	下午	7-2-5
afterwards	以後	以后	12-2-5
again	再	再	12-2-14
all, both	都	都	2-1-13
already	已經	已经	11-2-3
also	也	也	3-1-12
altogether	一共	一共	4-1-1
America	美國	美国	1-2-17
ancient times	古代	古代	8-2-3
and, as well as	和	和	3-1-8
annoying	討厭	讨厌	14-2-7
appetite	胃口	胃口	15-1-7
approximately	左右	左右	13-1-16
approximately, about, probably	大概	大概	9-1-9
arrive	到	到	11-1-12
to ask	問	问	7-2-19
at	在	在	6-2-5
aunt; here a polite term for a friend's mother regardless of age	伯母	伯母	2-2-2
autumn (season)	秋天	秋天	14-1-12
B			
back	後面	后面	6-1-12
bank	銀行	银行	7-1-9
baseball	棒球	棒球	3-1-7
basketball	籃球	篮球	3-1-11

English definition	Traditional Characters	Simplified Characters	Lesson-Dialogue-Number
bathroom	浴室	浴室	11-1-7
to be	是	是	1-1-6
to be able to, can	會	会	5-2-10
beautiful	美	美	6-1-9
because	因為	因为	10-2-16
beef	牛肉	牛肉	5-1-1
before	以前	以前	10-1-12
to begin, to start	開始	开始	7-2-15
birthday	生日	生日	13-1-1
blue	藍色	蓝色	10-2-15
book	書	书	2-2-5
both...and...	又	又	8-1-13
a bowl of	碗	碗	5-1-17
boy-, male-	男	男	10-2-8
brothers	兄弟	兄弟	2-2-12
bus	公共汽車（公車）	公共汽车（公车）	8-2-11
business	生意	生意	12-2-4
busy	忙	忙	7-2-10
to be busy, to be engaged	有事	有事	7-2-21
but, however	可是	可是	5-2-3
but, however	但是	但是	8-1-12
to buy	買	买	4-1-5
by the way	對了	对了	7-1-15
Bye. Take care.	慢走	慢走	14-2-17
C			
cable TV	有線電視	有线电视	11-2-17
cake	蛋糕	蛋糕	13-2-11
to be called, i.e., to have the first name xx	叫	叫	1-1-16
calligraphy	書法	书法	7-2-13
can, to be able to	能	能	4-2-8
to be careful, to take care	小心	小心	14-2-11
to catch/have a cold	感冒	感冒	15-1-13

English definition	Traditional Characters	Simplified Characters	Lesson-Dialogue-Number
to celebrate	過	过	13-1-15
cell phone	手機	手机	4-2-3
certainly, of course	當然	当然	13-1-8
character	字	字	7-2-16
cheap, inexpensive	便宜	便宜	4-2-13
China	中國	中国	8-2-10
Chinese language	中文	中文	3-2-12
Chinese last name, common in Taiwan	林	林	11-1-22
class	課	课	7-2-14
classmate	同學	同学	8-2-1
classroom	教室	教室	6-2-17
clean	乾淨	干净	10-2-12
clothes	衣服	衣服	10-2-5
coffee	咖啡	咖啡	1-2-14
cold	風	风	14-1-2
to come	來	来	1-1-5
to come back	回來	回来	13-1-3
comfortable	舒服	舒服	8-1-14
company	公司	公司	12-1-13
complement marker	得	得	5-2-9
to be concerned about	關心	关心	15-2-15
continuously, all the way	一直	一直	15-1-2
convenience store	便利商店	便利商店	8-1-20
convenient	方便	方便	6-2-2
to cook	做飯	做饭	5-2-8
correct, right	對	对	10-1-11
could (possibility)	可以	可以	3-2-10
could (possibility)	可以	可以	5-2-13
country	國家	国家	12-2-10
cuisine	菜	菜	3-2-16
cup	杯	杯	4-1-6

D

English definition	Traditional Characters	Simplified Characters	Lesson-Dialogue-Number
Da-an (name of a KTV named after a district in Taipei, where Shida is also located)	大安	大安	7-1-12
dad	爸爸	爸爸	2-1-20

English definition	Traditional Characters	Simplified Characters	Lesson-Dialogue-Number
date, day of a month	號	号	9-2-3
to decide	決定	决定	9-2-13
delicious	好吃	好吃	5-1-4
dessert	甜點	甜点	5-2-11
dinner	晚飯	晚饭	3-2-15
disposal marker	把	把	15-1-17
do what	做什麼	做什么	3-1-22
to do, to engage in	做	做	12-2-3
doctor	醫生	医生	15-1-1
Don't mention it. It's my pleasure.	哪裡，哪裡	哪里，哪里	13-2-14
don't (used in imperatives)	別	别	15-2-14
dormitory	宿舍	宿舍	6-2-11
downstairs	樓下	楼下	6-1-18
to drink	喝	喝	1-2-2

E

English definition	Traditional Characters	Simplified Characters	Lesson-Dialogue-Number
easy to	好	好	12-2-6
to eat	吃	吃	3-2-14
egg	蛋	蛋	13-2-7
the end of December	十二月底	十二月底	14-1-18
with enthusiasm	熱心	热心	13-1-12
even (more, less, etc.)	更	更	14-2-9
evening, night	晚上	晚上	3-2-3
every, each	每	每	7-2-11
everyone	大家	大家	14-2-10
Excellent. Great.	太好了	太好了	5-1-21
to exchange	交換	交换	13-1-10
to exercise	運動	运动	3-1-4
expensive	貴	贵	4-2-11
extra fine noodles	麵線	面线	13-2-6

F

English definition	Traditional Characters	Simplified Characters	Lesson-Dialogue-Number
to fall ill	生病	生病	15-1-11
family (members)	家人	家人	2-1-4
far	遠	远	6-1-6
fast	快	快	8-1-9
to feel, to think	覺得	觉得	3-1-15
few in number	少	少	5-1-6
film	影片	影片	9-1-5

English definition	Traditional Characters	Simplified Characters	Lesson-Dialogue-Number
fine, well	好	好	1-1-14
to finish	結束	结束	7-2-8
to finish class	下課	下课	7-2-4
first	先	先	12-1-5
five	五	五	2-2-14
to flow	流	流	15-1-3
for	幫	帮	4-1-13
for here	內用	内用	4-1-19
for, on behalf of	替	替	12-1-14
to forget	忘（了）	忘（了）	13-1-6
fragrant	香	香	10-1-6
friend	朋友	朋友	6-1-20
from	從	从	7-1-6
front	前面	前面	6-1-10
fruit	水果	水果	10-1-1
in the future	以後	以后	12-1-16

G

English definition	Traditional Characters	Simplified Characters	Lesson-Dialogue-Number
game, competition	比賽	比赛	7-2-7
gate, entrance	門口	门口	13-1-17
general measure word	個	个	2-2-10
to get	拿	拿	15-1-16
to get settled down, to get used to	習慣	习惯	11-2-4
gift, present	禮物	礼物	13-2-1
girl-, female-	女	女	9-2-1
to give	給	给	10-1-4
to give someone a ride to someone on / in a vehicle e.g. bicycle or car	載	载	8-2-6
to give it a try, to try and see what happens	試試看	试试看	12-2-15
to go	去	去	3-1-19
to go back, to return	回去	回去	11-1-17
go home	回家	回家	15-2-22
to go out	出去	出去	9-1-8
to go to class	上課	上课	6-1-21
to go to work	上班	上班	12-1-18
to go/come to	到	到	12-1-17

English definition	Traditional Characters	Simplified Characters	Lesson-Dialogue-Number
to go/stay with somebody, to accompany	陪	陪	15-2-7
Goodbye.	再見	再见	7-1-17
good-looking	好看	好看	2-1-16
grades	成績	成绩	12-1-11

H

English definition	Traditional Characters	Simplified Characters	Lesson-Dialogue-Number
half	半	半	7-2-6
happy	開心	开心	10-2-3
happy	快樂	快乐	13-1-2
Happy Birthday.	生日快樂	生日快乐	13-1-19
hard to, difficult to	難	难	12-2-12
to have	有	有	2-1-10
to have a fever	發燒	发烧	15-1-12
to have a holiday	放假	放假	9-1-10
to have a meal	吃飯	吃饭	6-2-10
to have a taste, try it, taste it	吃吃看	吃吃看	10-1-15
to have free time	有空	有空	7-1-16
to have fun	玩	玩	8-1-4
to have to, must	得	得	7-1-8
he, him	他	他	1-2-10
head	頭	头	15-1-5
health	健康	健康	15-2-9
health center	健康中心	健康中心	15-2-21
hear that	聽說	听说	6-1-23
here, this place	這裡	这里	6-2-3
High Speed Rail (HSR)	高鐵	高铁	8-1-18
home, house	家	家	2-1-5
homework	功課	功课	9-1-7
to hope	希望	希望	12-1-15
hot	熱	热	4-1-7
hot (spicy)	辣	辣	5-2-4
hotel	旅館	旅馆	10-2-6
hour	鐘頭	钟头	8-1-7
hour	小時	小时	15-2-18
house	房子	房子	2-1-7
how	怎麼	怎么	8-1-5

English definition	Traditional Characters	Simplified Characters	Lesson-Dialogue-Number
How about it? How does that sound? What do you think?	怎麼樣	怎么样	3-1-20
How about...? How does that sound?	好不好	好不好	3-2-18
How are you? Hello.	你好	你好	1-1-23
How come?	怎麼	怎么	13-1-5
how long	多久	多久	9-1-13
how many	幾	几	2-2-9
how much, how many	多少	多少	4-1-2
however, but	不過	不过	11-2-12
Hualien, name of a city on the eastern coast of Taiwan	花蓮	花莲	6-1-22
hundred	百	百	4-1-15

I

English definition	Traditional Characters	Simplified Characters	Lesson-Dialogue-Number
I, me	我	我	1-1-11
I'm sorry.	對不起	对不起	1-2-18
icy	冰	冰	15-2-13
if	要是	要是	9-2-14
to be inflamed	發炎	发炎	15-1-10
inside	裡面	里面	6-2-8
to install	裝	装	11-2-11
insurance	保險	保险	15-2-10
interesting, fun	好玩	好玩	3-1-16
to be interesting, to be fun	有意思	有意思	7-2-22
on the Internet	網路上	网络上	8-1-19
It would be best.../ (You) should···	最好	最好	15-2-23
It's not necessary.	不用了	不用了	15-2-20

J

English definition	Traditional Characters	Simplified Characters	Lesson-Dialogue-Number
Japan	日本	日本	1-2-16
job, work	工作	工作	12-2-8
just now	剛	刚	7-2-3

K

English definition	Traditional Characters	Simplified Characters	Lesson-Dialogue-Number
Karaoke	KTV	KTV	7-1-2
keep up the good work	加油	加油	12-1-22
to kick	踢	踢	3-1-13

English definition	Traditional Characters	Simplified Characters	Lesson-Dialogue-Number
kind, type	種	种	4-2-7
kitchen	廚房	厨房	11-1-4
to know	知道	知道	5-1-12

L

English definition	Traditional Characters	Simplified Characters	Lesson-Dialogue-Number
landlord	房東	房东	11-1-2
language	語言	语言	13-1-9
language center	語言中心	语言中心	12-1-21
large	大	大	4-1-10
last month	上個月	上个月	10-2-18
last time	上次	上次	14-2-16
last year	去年	去年	12-2-2
later	等一下	等一下	7-2-20
to laugh, to smile	笑	笑	10-2-2
to learn, to study	學	学	3-2-11
left (side)	左邊	左边	11-1-5
library	圖書館	图书馆	6-2-15
light repast, snack	小吃	小吃	5-1-8
to like	喜歡	喜欢	1-2-8
to listen	聽	听	3-1-2
living room	客廳	客厅	11-1-3
to be located at	在	在	6-1-3
long (time)	久	久	12-1-3
long time no see	好久不見	好久不见	13-1-21
to look for	找	找	12-2-7
lunch	午餐	午餐	7-2-2

M

English definition	Traditional Characters	Simplified Characters	Lesson-Dialogue-Number
to make a phone call	打電話	打电话	11-1-23
a man from Japan	田中誠一	田中诚一	2-2-1
a man from Taiwan	李明華	李明华	1-1-2
a man from the Republic of Honduras	馬安同	马安同	2-1-2
a man from the US	王開文	王开文	1-1-3
mango	芒果	芒果	10-1-3
many	多	多	2-1-11
Maokong, name of a must-see place in Taipei to visit for fine tea and scenery	貓空	猫空	9-2-16
Mass Rapid Transit (MRT)	捷運	捷运	8-2-7

English definition	Traditional Characters	Simplified Characters	Lesson-Dialogue-Number
may (permission)	可以	可以	7-2-18
May all your wishes come true.	心想事成	心想事成	13-2-17
May everything go your way.	萬事如意	万事如意	13-2-16
May I ask you..., Excuse me,⋯	請問	请问	1-1-20
measure word for bags, packages etc.	包	包	15-2-16
measure word for cell phones	支	支	4-2-1
measure word for Chinese money	塊	块	4-1-16
measure word for day	天	天	7-2-12
measure word for flat objects (e.g., paper, tickets)	張	张	2-1-15
measure word for houses, rooms, etc.	間	间	11-1-13
measure word for minutes	分鐘	分钟	11-1-10
measure word for pieces of food (e.g., meat, cake)	塊	块	10-1-5
measure word for times, occurrences	次	次	15-2-6
measure word for year	年	年	12-1-2
measure word for buildings	棟	栋	6-2-13
measure word for restaurants, shops, etc.	家	家	5-1-13
medicine	藥	药	15-1-14
medium	中	中	4-1-11
to meet	見面	见面	7-1-5
to meet, to see	找	找	6-1-19
to microwave	微波	微波	4-1-14
minute	分	分	7-1-4
to miss (someone)	想	想	14-1-6
Miss, Ms.	小姐	小姐	1-1-7
modification marker	的	的	2-1-3
mom	媽媽	妈妈	2-1-21
money	錢	钱	4-1-3

English definition	Traditional Characters	Simplified Characters	Lesson-Dialogue-Number
month of a year	月	月	9-2-2
(comparatively) more	比較	比较	8-1-8
morning	早上	早上	3-1-18
most	最	最	5-1-9
most (of), mostly	大部分	大部分	13-2-15
motorcycle, scooter	機車	机车	8-2-5
mountain	山	山	6-1-13
on a mountain, in the mountains	山上	山上	6-1-4
movie	電影	电影	3-2-5
Mr.	先生	先生	1-1-13
a multi-storey building	大樓	大楼	6-2-14
music	音樂	音乐	3-1-3

N

English definition	Traditional Characters	Simplified Characters	Lesson-Dialogue-Number
name	名字	名字	2-2-4
National Palace Museum	故宮博物院（故宮）	故宫博物院（故宫）	8-2-9
near	近	近	6-2-1
to need	需要	需要	12-1-8
new	新	新	4-2-2
New Year	新年	新年	14-1-7
New York	紐約	纽约	14-1-16
news	新聞	新闻	14-2-8
next time	下次	下次	7-1-13
next week	下個星期	下个星期	9-1-11
next year	明年	明年	14-1-11
night market	夜市	夜市	9-2-8
No need to stand on formalities, i.e., It's my pleasure.	不必客氣	不必客气	13-1-22
No problem.	沒問題	没问题	7-1-14
noodles	麵	面	5-1-2
noon	中午	中午	7-1-7
not	不	不	1-2-11
not	沒	没	2-2-11
Not a problem.	沒關係	没关系	11-2-16
not bad	不錯	不错	5-2-12
(here) to not like, to fear	怕	怕	5-2-5

English definition	Traditional Characters	Simplified Characters	Lesson-Dialogue-Number
not to look good	難看	难看	15-2-2
not well	不好	不好	5-2-17
now	現在	现在	6-1-16

O

English definition	Traditional Characters	Simplified Characters	Lesson-Dialogue-Number
O.K.	好啊	好啊	3-1-23
O.K.	好的	好的	4-1-17
O.K.	好	好	2-1-9
ocean	海	海	6-1-11
o'clock	點	点	7-1-1
often	常	常	3-1-10
oily, greasy	油	油	15-2-12
old	舊	旧	4-2-5
older brother	哥哥	哥哥	2-2-6
older sister	姐姐	姐姐	2-1-18
only, merely	就	就	11-1-11
only, merely	只	只	14-1-14
Oolong tea	烏龍茶	乌龙茶	1-2-15
opportunity	機會	机会	10-1-13
or	或是	或是	8-1-16
or (used in a question)	還是	还是	3-2-8
to order (meals)	點	点	5-1-16
to order (something in advance)	訂	订	13-2-3
outside	外面	外面	6-2-7

P

English definition	Traditional Characters	Simplified Characters	Lesson-Dialogue-Number
painful	痛	痛	15-1-6
parents	父母	父母	14-1-9
a particle indicating a realization	啊	啊	13-1-4
a particle used in addressing people, especially over the phone	喂	喂	11-2-1
to pay	付	付	11-2-13
person, people	人	人	1-2-7
a person's "color" (said of the face when healthy or sick, pleased or angry etc.)	臉色	脸色	15-2-1
pharmacy, drug store	藥局	药局	15-1-15
photo	照片	照片	2-1-12

English definition	Traditional Characters	Simplified Characters	Lesson-Dialogue-Number
to pick sb up	接	接	1-1-9
place	地方	地方	6-1-15
to plan to	打算	打算	9-1-3
to plan to	計畫	计划	12-1-1
to play (ball games)	打	打	3-1-5
please	請	请	1-2-1
Please come in!	請進	请进	2-1-22
poor, bad	差	差	15-1-8
pork knuckles	豬腳	猪脚	13-2-5
pretty	漂亮	漂亮	2-1-6
problem, question	問題	问题	11-2-5
progressive aspect verb; in the process of doing something	在	在	7-2-1

R

English definition	Traditional Characters	Simplified Characters	Lesson-Dialogue-Number
rain	雨	雨	14-2-1
to rain	下雨	下雨	14-2-14
to read	看書	看书	2-2-8
really	真	真	5-1-3
really must, definitely	一定	一定	5-1-15
really, truly	真的	真的	6-1-14
to receive	收到	收到	11-2-14
recently, lately	最近	最近	7-2-9
red	紅色	红色	10-1-8
red maple leaves	紅葉	红叶	14-1-13
to remember	記得	记得	13-1-7
to rent	租	租	11-1-1
rent (for a room or a house)	房租	房租	11-2-2
restaurant	餐廳	餐厅	5-2-2
to return to one's country	回國	回国	9-1-2
to ride	騎	骑	8-2-4
right (side)	右邊	右边	11-1-6
room	房間	房间	11-1-15

S

English definition	Traditional Characters	Simplified Characters	Lesson-Dialogue-Number
say	說	说	5-1-5
scary	可怕	可怕	14-2-12
scenery, landscape	風景	风景	6-1-8
scholarship	獎學金	奖学金	12-1-10

English definition	Traditional Characters	Simplified Characters	Lesson-Dialogue-Number
school	學校	学校	6-1-2
to see a doctor	看病	看病	15-2-8
to see, to watch	看	看	3-2-4
to seem to be, to appear to be (often used to take the edge off of a comment)	好像	好像	11-2-7
self	自己	自己	5-2-7
to sell	賣	卖	4-2-12
sentence final particle	嗎	吗	1-1-8
sentence final particle	呢	呢	1-2-9
sentence-final particle	啊	啊	3-1-21
sentence-final particle for guessing	吧	吧	10-1-10
sentence-final particle for suggestion	吧	吧	3-2-9
sentence-final particle indicating the speaker's sense of certainty	了	了	4-2-6
she, her	她	她	9-2-5
shop, store	店	店	5-1-14
short (height)	矮	矮	10-2-9
should	應該	应该	9-2-9
(by the) side, next to	旁邊	旁边	6-2-16
to sing	唱歌	唱歌	7-1-3
sisters	姐妹	姐妹	2-2-13
to sit	坐	坐	2-1-8
to ski	滑雪	滑雪	14-1-4
to sleep	睡覺	睡觉	15-1-20
to sleep	睡	睡	15-2-17
slow	慢	慢	8-1-6
small	小	小	4-1-12
snot, nasal mucus, a running nose	鼻水	鼻水	15-1-4
to snow	下雪	下雪	14-1-17
so	這麼	这么	5-1-11
so (very)	那麼	那么	13-1-11
soccer	足球	足球	3-1-14
sometimes	有時候	有时候	9-1-12
soon	快	快	14-1-8
sorry	不好意思	不好意思	11-2-15

English definition	Traditional Characters	Simplified Characters	Lesson-Dialogue-Number
soup, broth	湯	汤	5-1-10
Spain	西班牙	西班牙	13-1-18
the Spanish language	西班牙文	西班牙文	13-1-13
special	特別	特别	9-2-11
to spend (time or money)	花	花	12-1-9
spring (season)	春天	春天	14-1-5
station	站	站	8-1-15
to stay	住	住	10-2-17
steamed buns with meat stuffing filling	包子	包子	4-1-8
still, additionally	還	还	9-2-6
stinky tofu (fermented tofu)	臭豆腐	臭豆腐	5-1-20
stomach, abdomen	肚子	肚子	15-2-3
to stop	停	停	14-2-13
store, shop	商店	商店	6-2-9
store-owner, boss	老闆	老板	4-1-4
a storey, a floor	樓	楼	6-2-12
student	學生	学生	6-2-4
to study	念	念	12-1-6
to study	念書	念书	12-1-19
suggestion	建議	建议	9-2-7
suite, studio	套房	套房	11-1-16
summer (season)	夏天	夏天	14-2-5
supermarket	超市	超市	11-1-8
to be surnamed	姓	姓	1-1-15
sweet (taste)	甜	甜	10-1-7
to swim	游泳	游泳	3-1-9
swimming pool	游泳池	游泳池	6-2-18

T

English definition	Traditional Characters	Simplified Characters	Lesson-Dialogue-Number
Taiwan	臺灣 (＝台灣)	台湾 (＝台湾)	1-1-18
Tainan, a city in southwestern Taiwan	臺南	台南	8-1-17
Taitung, name of one of the major cities on the south eastern coast of Taiwan	臺東	台东	9-1-14
to take	帶	带	9-2-4
to take (pictures)	拍	拍	10-2-1

English definition	Traditional Characters	Simplified Characters	Lesson-Dialogue-Number
to take a photo	照相	照相	2-1-14
to take a rest	休息	休息	15-1-19
to take by, to travel by	坐	坐	8-1-1
take out, to go	外帶	外带	4-1-18
to take, to require	要	要	4-2-14
tall	高	高	10-2-10
(lit. good to drink) to taste good	好喝	好喝	1-2-5
taxi	計程車	出租车	8-2-13
tea	茶	茶	1-2-3
to teach	教	教	5-2-14
teacher	老師	老师	2-2-7
teahouse	茶館	茶馆	9-2-12
telephone	電話	电话	11-1-20
ten thousand	萬	万	4-2-15
tennis	網球	网球	3-1-6
(more...) than	比	比	8-2-8
thank you	謝謝	谢谢	1-1-22
that	那	那	4-2-10
that place, there	那裡	那里	6-1-7
That's right.	是啊	是啊	5-1-18
That's very kind of you.	太客氣	太客气	13-1-23
the day after tomorrow	後天	后天	7-1-11
the same, alike	一樣	一样	13-1-14
then	就	就	9-2-15
and then	再	再	11-1-19
then	那麼	那么	12-2-13
then, in that case	那	那	11-2-10
therefore, so	所以	所以	5-2-6
these	這些	这些	10-2-19
they (used for people only)	他們	他们	6-1-1
things, stuff	東西	东西	6-2-6
to think	想	想	11-1-18
this	這	这	1-1-12
(said of self on the phone) This is s/he speaking.	我就是	我就是	13-1-20
this kind (of)	這樣	这样	12-2-9

English definition	Traditional Characters	Simplified Characters	Lesson-Dialogue-Number
this time	這次	这次	14-2-15
this year	今年	今年	13-2-2
thousand	千	千	4-2-16
throat	喉嚨	喉咙	15-1-9
to throw up, to vomit	吐	吐	15-2-4
(train, bus) ticket	車票	车票	8-1-10
time	時間	时间	12-1-4
tired	累	累	12-1-20
to	到	到	5-2-15
to	給	给	11-1-21
to	對	对	13-2-12
to	跟	跟	15-2-11
today	今天	今天	3-2-2
together	一起	一起	3-2-13
tomorrow	明天	明天	3-1-17
too	太	太	4-2-4
toward, to	往	往	10-2-14
tradition, customs	傳統	传统	13-2-9
train	火車	火车	8-1-2
to travel	旅行	旅行	9-1-6
to treat sb to sth	請	请	10-1-14
to try	試	试	12-2-11
tuition	學費	学费	12-1-12
TV	電視	电视	9-1-4
two	兩	两	2-2-15
typhoon	颱風	台风	14-2-3
U			
umbrella	傘	伞	14-2-2
university	大學	大学	12-1-7
V			
vacant, empty	空	空	11-1-14
verbal particle indicating a completed action	了	了	13-2-4
very	很	很	1-2-4
very	非常	非常	8-1-11
vicinity, near	附近	附近	6-1-17
Vietnam	越南	越南	3-2-17
to visit (an institution)	參觀	参观	8-2-2

English definition	Traditional Characters	Simplified Characters	Lesson-Dialogue-Number
W			
to wait for	等	等	11-2-9
to walk	走路	走路	11-1-9
to wander around, to look around	逛	逛	9-2-10
to want to	要	要	1-2-13
to want, to need	要	要	4-1-9
to want, to think	想	想	3-2-7
water	水	水	15-1-18
water heater	熱水器	热水器	11-2-6
watermelon	西瓜	西瓜	10-1-9
we, us	我們	我们	1-1-10
to wear, to put on	穿	穿	10-2-4
weather	天氣	天气	14-1-1
week	星期	星期	9-1-1
weekend	週末	周末	3-1-1
welcome	歡迎	欢迎	1-1-19
well known, famous	有名	有名	5-1-7
wet	濕	湿	14-2-6
what	什麼	什么	1-2-6
What's wrong?	怎麼了	怎么了	15-2-19
when	時候	时候	7-1-10
where	哪裡	哪里	6-1-5
which	哪	哪	1-2-12
Which country?	哪國	哪国	1-2-19
who	誰	谁	2-1-17
why	為什麼	为什么	4-2-17
wife	太太	太太	10-2-7
will	會	会	11-2-8
will not do	不行	不行	8-2-12
will, be going to	要	要	14-2-4
wind	冷	冷	14-1-3
window	窗戶	窗户	10-2-13
winter (season)	冬天	冬天	14-1-10
to wish (somebody happiness, good luck, etc.)	祝	祝	13-2-13
with	跟	跟	8-1-3
a woman from Taiwan	張怡君	张怡君	2-1-1

English definition	Traditional Characters	Simplified Characters	Lesson-Dialogue-Number
a woman from the US	白如玉	白如玉	3-2-1
a woman from Vietnam	陳月美	陈月美	1-1-1
to work	工作	工作	12-2-1
to write	寫	写	7-2-17
X			
xiaolongbao, e.g., small meat and cabbagefilled steamed buns	小籠包	小笼包	5-1-19
Y			
yellow	黃色	黄色	10-1-2
yes	是的	是的	1-1-21
yesterday	昨天	昨天	5-2-1
you	你	你	1-1-4
you (female)	妳	妳	3-2-6
you (honorific)	您	您	2-2-3
you (plural)	你們	你们	1-1-17
You're welcome.	不客氣	不客气	1-1-22
young	年輕	年轻	13-2-10
younger brother	弟弟	弟弟	10-2-11
younger sister	妹妹	妹妹	2-1-19
Yu Shan (Mount Jade), tallest mountain in central Taiwan	玉山	玉山	14-1-15

简體字 课文参考 / Text in Simplified Characters

第一课　欢迎你来台湾！

对话一

明　华：请问 你是 陈月美 小姐 吗？
月　美：是的。谢谢 你 来 接 我们。
明　华：不客气。我是 李明华。
月　美：这是 王先生。
开　文：你好。我 姓 王，叫 开文。
明　华：你们好。欢迎 你们 来 台湾。

对话二

明　华：请 喝茶。
开　文：谢谢。很 好喝。请问 这是 什么 茶？
明　华：这是 乌龙茶。台湾 人 喜欢 喝茶。开文，你们 日本 人 呢？
月　美：他 不是 日本人。
明　华：对不起，你是 哪 国 人？
开　文：我是 美国人。
明　华：开文，你要 不要 喝 咖啡？
开　文：谢谢！我 不喝 咖啡，我 喜欢 喝茶。

第二课　我的家人

对话一

怡　君：这是 我家。请 进！
安　同：很 漂亮 的 房子！

[They enter Yijun's house.]

怡　君：请 坐！要 不要 喝茶？
安　同：好，谢谢 你。你家 有 很多 照片。
怡　君：我 家人 都 很 喜欢 照相。
安　同：这张 照片 很 好看。这是 谁？你 姐姐 吗？
怡　君：不是，是 我 妹妹。这是 我 爸爸、妈妈。
安　同：你 家人 都 很 好看。

对话二

明　华：田中，欢迎！欢迎！请 进。
田　中：谢谢。
明　华：田中，这是 我 妈妈。
田　中：伯母，您 好。
明华的妈妈：你好，你好。来！来！来！请 坐。你 叫 什么 名字？
田　中：我 叫 诚一。你们 家 有 很多 书。
明　华：都是 我 哥哥 的 书。他是 老师，他 很 喜欢 看书。
明华的妈妈：诚一，你家 有 几个 人？你 有没有 兄弟 姐妹？
田　中：我家 有 五个人，我 有 两个 妹妹。

第三课　周末做什么？

对话一

安　同：田中，你 喜欢 听 音乐 吗？
田　中：我 不喜欢 听 音乐。我 喜欢 运动。
安　同：你 喜欢 打 网球 吗？
田　中：我 不喜欢 打 网球。
安　同：你 喜欢 做 什么？
田　中：打 棒球 和 游泳，你 呢？
安　同：我 常 打 篮球，也 常 踢 足球。
田　中：我 觉得 踢 足球 很 好玩。
安　同：明天 是 周末，我们 早上 去 踢 足球，怎么样？
田　中：好 啊！

对话二

如　玉：今天 晚上 我们 去 看 电影，好 不 好？
月　美：好 啊！
如　玉：妳 想 看 美国 电影 还是 台湾 电影？
月　美：美国 电影、台湾 电影，我 都 想 看。
如　玉：我们 看 台湾 电影 吧！
月　美：好 啊！看 电影 可以 学 中文。
如　玉：晚上 要 不要 一起 吃 晚饭？
月　美：好，我们 去 吃 越南 菜。

第四课　请问一共多少钱？

对话一

老　板：请问 你要 买 什么？
明　华：一杯 热 咖啡。两个 包子。
老　板：你要 大杯、中杯 还是 小杯？
明　华：大杯。包子 请 帮 我 微波。
老　板：好的。请问 外带 还是 内用？
明　华：外带，一共 多少钱？
老　板：咖啡 八十，包子 四十，一共 一百 二十 块。

对话二

月　美：我 想 买 一支 新手机。
明　华：妳 的 手机 很好。为什么 要 买 新的？
月　美：我 这支 手机 太 旧了，不好看。
明　华：妳 想 买 哪种 手机？
月　美：能 照相 也 能 上网。
明　华：那种 手机 很好，我 哥哥 有 一支。
月　美：贵 不贵？一支 卖 多少钱？
明　华：那种 手机 不便宜。一支 要 一万 五千 多。

第五课　牛肉面真好吃

对话一

月　美：很 多 人 都 说 台湾 有 不 少 有名 的
　　　　小吃。
明　华：是 啊！牛肉面、小笼包、臭 豆腐…都
　　　　很 好吃。
月　美：你 最 喜欢 吃 什么？
明　华：牛肉 面。牛肉 好吃，汤 也 好喝。
月　美：这么 好吃，我 很 想 吃。
明　华：我 知道 一 家 有名 的 牛肉 面 店，我
　　　　们一起 去 吃，怎么样？
月　美：太 好 了！
明　华：我们 明天 去 。一定 要 点 大 碗 的。

对话二

月　美：昨天 晚上 那 家 餐厅 的 菜 很 好吃，
　　　　可是 有 一点 辣。
安　同：我 也 怕 辣，所以 我 喜欢 自己 做饭。
月　美：你 做饭 做 得 怎么样？
安　同：我 做 得 不好。妳 会 做饭 吗？
月　美：会。我 的 甜点 也 做 得 不错。
安　同：我 最 喜欢 吃 甜点。妳 可以 教 我 吗？
月　美：好的，这个 周末，你 到 我 家 来。
安　同：好 啊! 谢谢 妳。

Linking Chinese

當代中文課程　課本 1-1（二版）

策　　劃	國立臺灣師範大學國語教學中心	發 行 人	林載爵
主　　編	鄧守信	社　　長	羅國俊
顧　　問	Claudia Ross、白建華、陳雅芬	總 經 理	陳芝宇
審　　查	姚道中、葉德明、劉　珣	總 編 輯	涂豐恩
編寫教師	王佩卿、陳慶華、黃桂英	副總編輯	陳逸華
英文審查	李　櫻、畢永峨		

執行編輯	張莉萍、張雯雯、張黛琪、蔡如珮	叢書編輯	賴祖兒
英文翻譯	范大龍、張克微、蔣宜臻、龍潔玉	地　　址	新北市汐止區大同路一段 369 號 1 樓
校　　對	張莉萍、張雯雯、張黛琪、蔡如珮、李芃、鄭秀娟	聯絡電話	(02)8692-5588 轉 5305
		郵政劃撥	帳戶第 0100559-3 號
編輯助理	許雅晴、喬愛淳	郵撥電話	(02)23620308
技術支援	李昆璟	印 刷 者	文聯彩色製版印刷有限公司
插　　畫	何慎修、張榮傑、黃奕穎	2021 年 10 月初版 · 2024 年 3 月初版第八刷	
封面設計	Lady Gugu	版權所有 · 翻印必究	
內文排版	洪伊珊	Printed in Taiwan.	
錄　　音	王育偉、王品超、李世揚、吳霈蓁、馬君珮、許伯琴、Michael Tennant	ISBN	978-957-08-5963-8 (平裝)
		GPN	1011001469
錄音後製	純粹錄音後製公司	定　　價	400 元

著作財產權人　國立臺灣師範大學
地址：臺北市和平東路一段 162 號
電話：886-2-7749-5130
網址：http://mtc.ntnu.edu.tw/
E-mail：mtcbook613@gmail.com

感謝

王佩卿、王盈婷、王盈雯、何瑞章、李尚遠、林欣穎、林聖雄、林嫣芳、林蔚儒、徐國欽、張素華、
張瑜庭、莊淑帆、陳宇婕、陳冠引、陳建宏、陳昱蓉、陳韋誠、陳書韋、陳淑美、陳逸達、陳嘉禧、
陳鳳儀、傅聖芳、黃奕穎、楊凌雁、虞永欣、蔡宛蓉、賴瑩玲
協助拍攝本教材及試用教材期間使用之相關照片

udn TV、中央氣象局、《中國顏色》（黃仁達／著、攝）、台北 101、台灣大車隊、
《台灣喫茶》（吳德亮／著、攝）、統一超商、蕙風堂、聯合報
授權提供本教材之相關照片

（以上依姓氏或單位名稱筆畫順序排列）

國家圖書館出版品預行編目資料

當代中文課程 課本1-1（二版）/國立臺灣師範大學國語
教學中心策劃．鄧守信主編．初版．新北市．聯經．
2021年10月．148面．21×28公分（Linking Chiese）
ISBN 978-957-08-5963-8（平裝）
2024年3月初版第八刷

1.漢語 2.讀本

802.86 110012624